I'VE BEEN A NAUGHTY GIRL

by
Dahlia Schweitzer

THE BAO HOUSE
TORONTO * LOS ANGELES * NEW YORK CITY

I've Been A Naughty Girl
By Dahlia Schweitzer

Copyright © 2013 Dahlia Schweitzer

Introduction

I am a girl who loves sex. I am also a girl who loves writing. But it never occurred to me to combine the two until years after my B.A. in English made me at home within the realm of pure academic writing. Because that's what I did. I didn't make stuff up, I broke it down.

Then, one night, after a crazy adventure in a nightclub on the west side of Manhattan, I spewed the tale of my adventures into email format, for the entertainment of an old college friend. His response? "Turn this into a story!" "I don't write stories," I explained. "I dissect Shakespeare."

He didn't care, and, most importantly, he didn't let up. The (slightly) fictionalized adaptation of that night's adventures became my first short story—and no, I won't tell you which one it was. One of the things I discovered about making stuff up is that no one can tell when you're not. In other words, I am the only one who can separate the fact from the fiction, the real life experiences from the purely imaginative, the super secret fantasies that rouse me from my late afternoon naps (or send me to them) from the more cerebral "what would happen if she did this and then he did that?" No one else knows.

Seduce Me came first. It came in fits and starts, never gaining the momentum of confidence, as I wrote on a whim, on occasion, when life permitted or encouraged it. Who knew, after all, if these stories would ever go anywhere? So it was as shocking to me as it was to my mother when the collection was published, together, as a proud unit, not orphaned into anthologies. Not only did people like my stories, but they liked them enough to buy them *together*.

It was with a frantic flurry of excitement and determination that I wrote its sequel, *I've Been a Naughty*

5

Girl. Unlike its predecessor, it was not spaced out over the course of two years. It was cranked out. I couldn't stop. I put my life on hold, locked myself up in my mother's extra bedroom, and wrote. Every day. Telling the stories that filled my fantasies and imagination while my actual life was focused and absolute. All I did was write. Suddenly, I had an audience. I had to create a product.

When I couldn't write, I watched movies, my head constantly distracted by the trials and tribulations of my respective protagonists, by their desires, which, in turn, became mine. As often happens when I write, I ate a lot of ice cream and carbohydrates. I went for long walks. And I took a lot of, ahem, naps.

During those long stretches of solitude, my imagination kept me company. Ex-lovers, current lovers, wanna-be lovers, imaginary lovers—they were all there in my head, living, breathing, and, most importantly, lusting.

I am a girl who likes sex, who likes to explore it, physically, intellectually and cerebrally. Sex means different things to different people, but for me it's always had a very powerful effect on my identity, and my search to understand myself. Women who are comfortable with sex, with having it, asking for it, and talking about it, inhabit a unique place in this world. They are often judged. They are occasionally feared.

In my stories, I write about women who are not afraid to ask for what they want, and about men (or other women) who are turned on by these demands. I write about women who love sex, love having it, and aren't afraid to take control.

While some of the adventures are based on my personal experiences, and some of the characters are based on people I've met, my protagonists are always a little undefined. They're often unnamed. Maybe she is me…but maybe she is you?

Contents

DAHLIA SCHWEITZER

101

He couldn't have said what it was that made her catch his eye. It certainly wasn't her makeup, which had been applied with the vigor of a twelve year old attending her first party, or her dress, whose virginal emphasis banished any thoughts of provocation behind its awkward stiffness or childish puffiness—or maybe it was?

Maybe it was precisely how she glowed, despite the weight of her poorly strategized attire, the flush of her cheeks and blueness of her eyes that managed to stand out even underneath the makeup, which left him unable to take his eyes off her. Him, a guy who could have had any girl in the room—but his gaze kept drifting back to her as she drifted through the party, looked just a little bit lost and just a hell of a lot adorable.

Knowing she had to be a freshman, knowing what it would do to him and his reputation, he couldn't help it—he crossed the room and offered her a drink.

She accepted it and his attentions gratefully. Eyes demure, cheek flush enhanced, and cleavage rising and falling even faster. Again, he couldn't help it—he felt himself staring as his grip on his plastic cup tightened and he studied the fall of her long blonde hair. He wanted to see her with her clothes off. He wanted to feel those breasts under his hands. He wanted to rip off that horrid dress and sit her down, on top of him, naked, sweating, riding him up and down, breasts, those big soft beautiful breasts bouncing above her tiny waist.

He flushed when he realized she was still talking to him, and he hadn't heard a word.

"Sorry, darlin', what's that?" With colossal effort, he

pulled his eyes up and focused them on hers. On her big beautiful blue eyes despite the green stuff she'd outlined them in. My god, where did this girl come from…and did she belong to anyone? He glanced around the room but no one seemed to be paying either of them the slightest bit of attention.

"I was just asking if you're in my AmLit class?"

He grinned at her. She was cute. "You're in AmLit 101?"

"Yeah! Are you?" Her smile was almost too much for him to bear. He clenched the plastic cup a little bit tighter, feeling it crack between his fingers and the remnants of beer drip onto his hand. He laughed, both to relieve the unfamiliar nervousness and because the situation itself *was* funny.

"I'm a senior, babe. I took that class several years ago."

"Oh. Sorry." She blinked at him. "I didn't know."

"That's okay. Don't worry about it. Can I get you another drink?"

"Sure!"

He smiled back at her. Now they were back on familiar territory, he thought, whisking her off in the direction of the bar.

With the ease of a professional, and the strategist of a true player, it didn't take long (it took just as long as expected, actually) before the requisite number of drinks had been served (and consumed), before the requisite number of jokes had been delivered (and laughed at), before the requisite number of compliments had been given (and blushingly accepted), and before they were on their way to Jim's room.

It was only when they got to Jim's room that he realized things might take a little longer than accepted. See, the funny thing is, her outfit really was sincere—this girl was straight off the Iowa cornfields. She was a virgin. And not only was she a virgin, but she told Jim, with nervous shyness, that she'd never even really been kissed before.

"You've never been kissed before?"

"I mean, I've been kissed before, but I've never, you know, *really* been kissed before. Like they do in the movies…" Her hands were nervously kneading patterns into the skirt of her dress, her eyes had long since been fixated on the floor, and Jim didn't know whether to laugh or cry.

A virgin? He didn't want to deal with a virgin. My god, he didn't have time for that. But he wanted this girl. Wow, how he wanted this girl. And the more he watched her nervously bite her lip, the more he wanted to bite it for her. And the more her breasts rose up and down as her breathing nervously accelerated, the more he wanted to release them from that damn awful dress and see them for how they really looked.

Well, he consoled himself, just because she hadn't done any of this stuff before, didn't mean she didn't want to, right?

"Just because you haven't done any of this stuff before, doesn't mean you don't want to, does it?"

"Oh god, no, oh no no. Of course I'd love to, it's just that, I don't know, it just, never, oh, I don't know—"

As good a time as any, Jim thought, as he went in for the kill, and yes, those lips tasted as delicious as they looked, as he pressed his against hers and ran his tongue into her sweet and beer-tasting mouth.

But then she jerked her head back and he flinched.

"Did I do something wrong?"

"Oh, no, it's not, I mean, is it supposed to feel like that?"

He stared. "Is what supposed to feel like what?"

"Is that what they do? In the movies? I mean, your tongue goes in my mouth? Like that?"

He laughed. "You've really never done this before?"

Her blush threatened to turn her cheeks the color of the fire engine he built when he was six.

She shook her head, kneading the blanket again.

Wow. He was in shock. But, at the same time, he couldn't help admitting that this was kind of fun. Not that it was really an ego boost, per se, but still, to be this girl's first kiss? Her first everything? That was certainly more intense than anything he'd done in a while. And for now, the novelty compensated for his customary lack of patience.

"It's ok. We'll go slow. I'll show you how it's done."

"And you won't laugh?" Her eyes looked up at him from behind huge lashes.

He blinked. For a second there, he really thought she was wearing blue mascara. Where did she come from? The bitchy side to his personality briefly wondered when he could ask her to wash her face, but then hormones took over and his brain returned to the task at hand.

"No. I won't laugh. Just relax. Open your mouth a little. Let me slip my tongue in there…actually, wait. I'm going to open *my* mouth a little, and I want you to slip *your* tongue in mine."

"For real?"

"Yes. For real. I promise, it feels good." He grinned at her. "Go as slow as you like. Enjoy it."

With that, he leaned over, jaw and lips relaxed, and let her mouth come to his.

At first, she was barely there…just sort of hovering on the edges, cautious, feeling, tasting, but then, gradually, as her confidence increased, she came closer, and her tongue slipped inside his mouth. He froze. Afraid to move, afraid that he'd scare her away like a little mouse, he tried not to show any reaction as her tongue timidly explored his lips, his teeth, his tongue—and then, ever-so-slowly, he reached forward, wrapping first one arm and then another around her waist, pulling her to him.

Her body was as warm as her mouth.

He smiled to himself, careful not to move his mouth too

much, and let his tongue slide between her lips. She didn't pull away, and he felt his confidence, like hers, increasing. Her mouth was perfect, and he didn't want to leave it. He could taste her lip gloss (Raspberry? Cherry?), and he reveled in the nostalgia of the moment, remembering his first kiss in the back of that movie theater and the taste of that lip gloss as though it were yesterday.

He ran his tongue along the line of her teeth, and she laughed.

"I can't believe this is how it's done."

"Why's that?"

"Oh, I don't know. Your tongue in my mouth, my tongue in yours. It's like we're eating each other. What's that got to do with love?"

"Everything. Haven't you ever thought something looked good enough to eat?"

She smiled. "You're right."

"And you most certainly do…"

With a line like that, he figured he'd set the stage for the kill. Leaning forward, one finger traced the line of her jaw, down her neck, and between those incredible breasts. One step closer to getting rid of that awful dress, he thought, and one step closer to feeling those breasts in his hands. Bringing the other hand around, encircling her waist, he tried to figure out the best way to progress.

"Is there a zipper on this thing?" he whispered in her ear.

"Wha- what's that?" she asked (full volume) pulling back sharply. "What did you ask?"

"Shh, it's okay. I just asked if your dress had a zipper?"

"Oh no, oh no, I don't want to take my dress off." But then, as if recognizing the harshness of her statement, she looked down and then up again, shaking her head ever so slightly, and, more demurely, "at least, not tonight."

Ah ha, so this is how we play the game, Jim thought.

He'd been here before, and even this was going to take a bit longer than normal, he knew how to do this. That dress was going to come off, it was just going to be a little more time than he'd originally bargained. But that was okay. Despite the growing tightness in his pants, he had all night. Jim was the kind of guy who believed in follow-through. Once he knew what he wanted, his eyes stayed focused on the ball. He was going to be there—as long as it took.

"Alright. Darling. We don't have to take your dress off. But do you mind if I take my shirt off? I'm getting a little hot over here…"

"Oh no. Of course. I mean, yes, sure, whatever you like. It's your room, do whatever you want." She laughed, a bit shyly, a bit nervously, and ever so sweetly.

Feeling like a Chippendale centerpiece, Jim slowly stretched his polo shirt over his head, exposing his quarterback arms and his self-consciously chiseled abs. As predicted, her eyes got a little bit bigger and her breasts heaved a little bit more, and, trying to keep the coolness in his voice, Jim patted the space on the bed next to him.

"Why don't you come sit closer?"

She smiled nervously.

"But my dress stays on?"

"Of course! What do you think? I'm going to rip it off?" With a mock growl, he leaned over, grabbed her around the waist, and pulled her towards him.

She giggled but did not resist.

Now they were sitting on the bed, hip to hip, thigh to thigh, waist to waist—faces inches apart. Jim attempted another kiss as his hand rested on her thigh.

She did not resist.

His hand slowly reached its way up her thigh, as the skin got warmer and smoother, and just as he felt as though he might slip into something dark and wet and oh so reassuring, her hand came down, resting upon his, and freezing it into position.

The kissing didn't stop, though.

He took solace in that, enjoying the feeling of her lips, her tongue, and especially enjoying the growing confidence he could feel in her body, in her movements, and in the way her hand slowly relaxed its pressure on his. Deciding to take a chance, he tried, once again, to inch his hand slightly further up her thigh. She allowed him another two inches before, once again, clenching down and slightly shaking her head.

The kissing still didn't stop—and Jim decided to switch tactics and try the other hand. It was his right hand that was on her thigh, his left hand that circled her waist. With the smoothness of a professional, that second hand made its way up over her ribs, curving inwards, until it lightly cupped her left breast.

Home run, he thought to himself, grinning inwardly, and that breast was just as perfect as he'd imagined. Just as large, just as luscious, and just as straining against the confines of the dress as his cock was straining in his pants. The time would come, the time would come, indeed.

As if she could hear his inner dialogue, not only did she not shift his hand off her breast, but she seemed to take it as a cue to reach her right hand around his waist, pressing their bodies even closer together.

Overflowing with confidence, right hand scooted up another inch.

She did not resist, and Jim, in his head, did a victory dance. This might have been ninth grade for its juvenile pleasures, but, man, this girl was better than anything he'd had back then, and he was willing to wait for what was proving to be a very delicious reward.

Coasting on the thrill of accomplishment, Jim decided to do a full-on breast feel, the kind he was more accustomed to giving. He ran his hand over, under, and around the breast, feeling the nipple growing harder, more pronounced through the fabric. Grabbing it between his fingers, he pulled gently, then slightly more firmly, as her moans provided all the encouragement he needed.

It was time to step it up a notch.

Briefly sad for ending the moment, but focused on the long-term goal, Jim leaned his head back, looking her in the eyes as the two of them each inhaled slowly, and then he curved his head down, kissing the breast through the fabric. She moaned again. He kissed harder. She moaned larder.

Time for more action.

He reached his left hand up further, grabbing the top edge of her dress, pulling it down as far as it would go. It didn't go far, but it went just enough—just enough to expose a brilliantly pink and hard nipple in the middle of a breast pressing firmly against the tight elastic. It seemed almost tragic to watch the breast suffering so, but all things came to those who wait. For now, he wanted the nipple.

Leaning over, he slipped her nipple into his mouth. Her moan mixed with a long exhale as she seemed to sag against him, and he flicked his tongue against the tip of the nipple, pressing his teeth gently along its base, left hand still pulling the edge of the dress down as far as it would go. It was so hard, so firm, and the breast so soft and still so heavy in his mouth—he wanted more.

His left hand tugged harder.

The two of them heard the crack at the same time.

"Oh no, my dress is going to rip."

"God, I'm sorry," he replied, jerking up apologetically. "I didn't mean, I mean, I'm sorry."

She smiled ruefully. "It's okay. It's kind of my fault, too."

"Is there a zipper? I mean, do you mind? Can we…?

16

She sighed. "It's okay. There's a zipper."

He reached forward.

"No, I'll do it. Let me."

She reached underneath her right armpit and tugged. The zipper was there?! No wonder he hadn't found it. And, of course, in fitting with the events of the evening, it wasn't one of those zippers that just slid the dress right off. It was just one of those underarm zippers which make it easier to pull a dress over one's head. He silently cursed dress manufacturers, but did notice, gratefully, that at least it had relieved enough pressure to expose one beautiful left breast.

With that left breast cupped in his left hand, he slipped his right hand up another inch. Sweating like a shoplifter, he felt almost euphoric at getting off scott free. Not only did she not rebuke, she started to kiss the side of his neck, licking the skin like a seductive pussycat. It took all his self-control not to throw her on her back on the bed and tear off the dress. He wanted her desperately, but this would not come so easy. He knew exactly how she'd react if he moved too fast, and he was not willing to give this one up yet.

His senses split every which way, part of his body relishing every touch of her tongue, another part enjoying the feeling of that one breast and dreaming of the other, while the focus of his efforts switched to that precious area on her thigh. That new inch of terrain that he'd recently been allowed to discover. While not moving any of his other fingers (in case she might force a retreat), he began to slide his thumb back and forth, back and forth, across her silky smooth skin.

Going for broke—after all, as she licked his neck and bit his ear, she wasn't exactly complaining—he sent his thumb (and the rest of the hand) up another inch, and then another, and then pay dirt.

He'd reached underwear.

And it was wet.

17

And she wasn't resisting!

He ran his fingers over the cotton fabric. A thong this was not, but it didn't matter. At this point in time, he didn't care what underwear she was wearing, he just wanted to know how long until it came off.

She was leaking through the material, and it drove him crazy to imagine what she felt like underneath, what she would feel like inside. He started to slip his fingers against the elastic edge, and slowly, slowly—until her hand came down like an enforcer.

"My underwear's not coming off," she whispered in his ear, between nibbles and kisses.

He was being driven truly crazy, between her touches, her breasts, the wetness of the underwear, and the fact that she still hadn't put her hand between his legs. His cock ached, neglected and constricted. But what could he do? These were her rules, and he had to play the game. He knew what would happen if he took it too far, too fast, and he wasn't willing to give up on his prize. He'd get there—in the end.

"That's okay," he whispered back, "but can't I just feel you?"

She thought for a second and then released her grip on his hand. He smiled and pulled her even closer with his left arm, while his right went in for the kill. Oh god, she was wet. Even durable cotton underwear couldn't absorb all of this. He didn't even know how to describe the sensation. He'd never felt like anything like this before. It wasn't silk, because it was too wet. But it wasn't a sloppy wet. It was a pure, sensuous wet. Deep, swollen, and, most amazingly, spread open, welcoming and inviting.

He took it gently first, just running his fingers back and forth, and then he began the slow clitoral circles as she shuddered, hot breath on his ear, fingers digging into his waist, until he slid one finger in—slowly, he didn't know if this was

18

her very first time—and she tightened, curved, and pressed against him.

"Does it feel good?" he asked, partly to check, and partly just to hear her answer.

"Uh huh," she panted. "Go slow, but please don't stop."

He had no intention of it. Alternating between one finger inside, angling up to stroke her g-spot, and making light circles along her increasingly swollen clitoris, until she made him stop.

"Tell me," she asked, "have you done this to lots of girls?"

"What do you mean?"

"You know, done *this*." She gestured downward with her head. "With lots of girls?"

He knew what she meant, but he didn't know how to answer. "I guess I've done it with a few?"

She laughed. "Are you asking me?"

"Asking you?"

"Yeah. You made it sound like a question."

"Oh." He laughed, too. "Sorry. It wasn't a question. It was, just, oh, I didn't know how to answer, so I guess I was asking if my answer was alright."

"Was your answer the truth?"

He paused. "Well, yes."

She smiled broadly. "So then, yes, your answer was alright. I mean, I know that you've done it with more people than I have. It's not hard to have more than zero! But I was just curious if it had been a lot." Her face turned sad. "I guess it has."

Tilting her face upwards with the hand that been between her legs but now had to serve other more serious purposes, he looked her in the eyes. Her beautiful eyes. She stared back at him.

Jim grinned. "Listen. I want to do what it takes to make

you feel comfortable, and I certainly want to make you feel good, so why don't you tell me what you need?"

"What I need?"

"Yeah. What'll make you feel more comfortable, with, with this."

Looking pensive, she glanced down for a minute. "Can we really do what I want?"

"Yeah, sure, of course. Sure. What do you want?"

"Can we lie down?"

"Totally. Of course."

Jim instantly leapt up to display a flurry of activity. In less than a minute, pillows, blanket, girl and boy were neatly arranged in horizontal position. He turned to look at her expectantly. She looked back at him. Turning to his side, he reached over and placed one hand gently on her thigh.

"Can we talk a little first?" she asked timidly.

Startled, he moved to take his hand back. She rested her hand on top of his, holding it there.

"It's ok. You can leave it there. I just, it's just, I feel like I don't know you at all."

"What would you like to know?"

"What are you most afraid of? What makes you most happy?"

Jim thought for a moment. "I guess. I'm most afraid of being alone… And what makes me most happy? I don't know. I don't know if I can say just one thing. Maybe music? Playing music?"

"Playing music? What do you play?"

"Guitar."

She nodded to herself as her fingers wrapped around his hand, and he watched the rise and fall of her chest.

Then, with a movement of quick impulsivity, she rolled over on top of him, one hand on either side of his neck, and looked him in the eyes. He laughed back at her, wrapped his arms around her waist, and pulled her down, mouth onto mouth, lips against lips.

Kissing like they do in the movies, Jim almost forgot what he was dealing with, and she almost forgot that there was anything to deal with. She tasted sweet and warm, and his kisses were soft and delicate, and both of them kissed intensely, as they pressed against each other. The pressure of his cock pushed harder at the fabric behind his zipper, and, subconsciously, he, in turn, pushed harder against her. She, subconsciously, started to spread her legs.

He took that as the catalyst to flip her onto her back. They looked at each other for a second, and then he slid his body down between her legs.

"Oh, no, I don't know…what are you going to do?" She started to lift her head and shoulders up, looking down at him.

He looked up and pressed one finger lightly against her red lips. "I won't take them off. I promise. Just let me…?"

With a sigh of nervousness, she leaned back on the bed and inhaled deeply. As she exhaled, he watched her chest fall, and took a deep breath himself. And then he put his face between her legs.

As she felt his warm breath, he could feel her start to relax, but relaxing isn't quite the right word for what happened once he gently stretched the underwear aside with his right hand and leaned a little forward, tenderly kissing her clitoris, her labia, the outer lips, her inner lips, starting with light kisses that gradually picked up pressure and speed, as the licking of the tongue began to replace the lips.

When he glanced up, he could see the chest's quickening pace as her breath grew shallower and her hands grabbed the blanket on either side in little fists. Jim flicked his tongue across her clitoris, and she released the tiniest little moan. He grinned, placing the palm of his hand on the soft mound of her pubic hair, resting his fingers lightly on her vaginal lips.

Lightly, slowly, he began to move his hand in tiny circles as her skin slid gently beneath.

He looked over at her, but she hadn't moved. Her fists still clenched the bed, her eyes were closed, her jaw even a little set, but there was the hint of a smile on her lips, and he smiled again.

"Everything okay?" he whispered.

"Uh huh."

"Want me to keep going?"

"Uh huh."

He nodded to himself. No problem with that. He could certainly do that.

He began to pull gently on one lip and then another, exploring the inner and outer lips with his fingers, rubbing first one then another gently between his forefinger and thumb. Then, slowly, carefully, watching for any sign of protest, he inserted one finger into her vagina. Just a little, just an inch or two, but she still flinched, reaching her hand over to grab him around the wrist.

"Oh god, I don't know."

"Let me try…if it hurts, I'll stop."

Pause. She said nothing, so he continued.

"Does it feel good so far?"

She nodded, saying nothing.

He smiled again. She smiled timidly back at him.

"Tell me if this feels good to you."

He pushed his index finger in deeper until his thumb rested against her clitoris. He began to move his thumb in even circles.

"Oh my god," was all she said, as her eyes closed again, and her head fell back on the pillow.

You have no idea, he thought to himself. This was just the beginning…

His thumb went round and round as he began to pull his

finger in and out with a steady motion. The deeper he went, the more she arched around him, the faster he went, the more her breath quickened, and he could feel her muscles clenching around his fingers, the blood rushing to the area, pulsing in the vessels, swelling and swelling as his cock swelled in his pants, and it was all he could do not to come in his own pants, so turned on was he by the sight of her on the bed, one breast exposed, chest heaving, legs spread wide (and then even wider), her liquid glittering on his hand, his finger going in and out of her pussy, her mouth open, breath shuddering in and out between those lips until her legs tightened, her fists clenched, her toes pointed, and then, as everything froze, suddenly, as though a switch were flicked, she collapsed, every muscle relaxed, several breaths worth of air exhaled through her lips.

"Stop. Oh god stop," she begged, grabbing his hand in hers. "It's too intense."

"No more?"

"No. No more. It's too…it's too much. Wait. Let me get my breath."

He smiled at her disarray, at the mess of confused stimuli rushing through her body. He slipped his finger back out, letting the underwear's elastic finally spring back to position.

"Come. Lay down," she said, patting the bed beside her.

Happy to comply with any of her requests, Jim lay down and put his arms around her, lying in silence as she collected her breath and her composure.

"My god, that was…beyond words." She laughed nervously, suddenly conscious of her exposed vulnerability. "Thank you."

He laughed. "You're very welcome."

She grabbed his hand in hers and squeezed it—twice—as they returned to the silence of their breaths, until she opened her mouth again hesitantly.

"I'd like to, I'd like to, give you something back."

"What do you mean?"

"You know, I'd like to do something for you. In exchange. You know."

"Oh, that's okay. We're not keeping score."

Flipping over on her stomach to stare him in the eyes, she said, "I know that. But I want to. I want to. But." She looked down, nervously. "I just don't know. I mean, I'm not going to be very good. I don't really know…Will you tell me? Will you give me instructions? Will you tell me when it's good? And when it's not?"

Her big eyes looked back at his. He grinned back.

"Sure. We can do it like that. It'll be fun."

"Yeah? You think?" She smiled. "You won't laugh?"

"Nah. I won't laugh. I'm sure whatever you do will feel good."

"Don't watch, though, okay?"

"Deal."

Then, after one more nervous glance at his eyes, she reached for his belt buckle.

Jim saw nothing, per her instructions, despite the fact that he desperately wanted to watch the trail of blond hair make its way down his stomach, following the path of wet kisses, down his chest, stopping briefly around each of his nipples, over his stomach, pit stops at each of his hips, running her fingers over the protrusion of bone, until she was finally, *finally* there, and oh god, he wanted to watch but he didn't dare, for fear that the slightest indication that he wasn't following her instructions would make her stop, and that—that was more important than whether or not he could see.

He couldn't believe that she'd never done this before. He couldn't believe the significance of beginner's luck. He couldn't believe how good it felt.

With the kind of skill that belongs only a girl who really

enjoys her work, she ran her tongue up and down the length of his cock, stopping each time at the tip to lick a circle around the circumference, and then sending the wet caress back to the base, up and down, up and down, dizzying Jim until he didn't care if the world ended or began as long as she didn't stop.

Up and down, up and down, with not really enough pressure for anything to actually happen, other than for him to get slowly harder and harder and harder, each time praying for her to let him deeper into her throat and each time feeling on the verge of losing consciousness when she ran her tongue across his tip. Up and down and up and down until he couldn't stand it any more. Until the feather light pressure of her tongue made him want to scream for more. Until he really felt like he was going to die if she didn't give him more.

"Can you try using your hand?" he said, as calmly as he could manage, hoping desperately that she wouldn't see his request as a criticism and stop all together.

(Luckily, she didn't.)

"Using my hand?" she replied, looking up, startled. "Like this?"

She took hold of his balls in her hand, and he thought he was going to die from the mixture of pleasure and pain.

"No, no," he said, wincing from the intensity of the sensation.

"I don't understand. I'm sorry, I thought it was meant to be…"

He smiled at her. "Everything you do feels good, just I meant like *this.*"

He gently wrapped her hand around the base of his cock with just enough tension to pull the skin back, leaving the tip a little more exposed, a little more sensitive, and then he showed her how to move her hand, how to slide it back and forth so that the skin shifted like layers of silk, and then he told her how it killed him when she used her mouth, and how much he'd love it if she could manage to do both.

Which, of course, she could, because, more than anything, she wanted to show Jim how good she could make him feel, and also because, despite her nervousness and first-timer's anxiety, she was kind of enjoying herself.

It took a little while until she got the hang of it—although he didn't seem to mind one way or another, as she was pleased to note—but after some practice, a couple times where she forgot to move her hand, or got so distracted by the smoothness of his skin, and the hypnotic way it slid back and forth, that she forgot to move her mouth, just letting it rest with the tip of his cock on the roof of her mouth, after that…after that, she felt like the majorette in a marching band, adeptly managing to do so many things at once without dropping any of them.

As soon as the rhythm of it all became unconscious, when the speed and movement of his pulsing veins matched that moving through hers, when she got her brain suspended just enough that it was sensation rather than thought dictating her actions, then it was almost easy. Movement of hand with machine accuracy, up and down, never failing speed, more heart and feeling in the mouth, in the lips, and the tongue which dripped all over the tip of his cock, faster and faster, as she began to feel almost euphoric, adrenaline rushed from the tension of his thighs into the tension of her body, until,

"I'm…I'm…" he said, and then he took hold of her head gently between his hands, pulling her face up to his.

"What's wrong?" she asked, her lips appearing swollen to twice their normal size and so wet and luscious, he wanted to eat them, but he settled for kissing them instead, a kiss so sweet, he felt like he'd never tasted anything like it.

"Is it alright?" she asked, pulling her head back, eyes staring at his with a look of total concern.

"Baby, it was amazing. Thank you. Thank you so much.

26

It was really perfect, only, only, I don't know, it didn't feel right to come in your mouth."

"Oh, but I was ready for it. I was waiting for it." She glanced down, embarrassed. "I kind of wanted to know what you would taste like."

"Really?" he stared at her, astonished.

She grinned. "Yeah. Is that silly of me?"

He grinned back. "Not at all. It's kind of sweet, actually."

"I am or that's what you taste like?" She laughed.

"Ha ha. Very funny." He grabbed her around the waist and pulled her down on top of him. "No more jokes. Kiss me."

They kissed and groped and rubbed and stroked and did all the things drunk college kids do when hormones have taken over their brains and all they feel is desire and lust and need, and everything appears to have a direct cause and effect to when he moves there or she touches there or he breathes there or she claws there. The kissing wasn't about lips or tongues anymore but about full body contact, and who could consume who, and who could pull whom tighter, and he wrapped his arms around her, trying to press himself against her, trying to rub his aching, swollen cock against any part that felt appropriate, while her underwear felt as damp as a flag in a rainstorm, and every time his hands ran across the fabric, she moaned and arched against him, and this continued with neither party knowing quite what to do next or quite how to satisfy what threatened to envelop them.

Until she pushed her left palm against the center of his upper chest, and said, "Stop. My turn." And then, with the confidence of one who knew her command would be obeyed, she slipped back down between his legs.

This time it was even better. This time, her hand was firmer, her tongue wetter, her lips softer, her mouth hotter, the rhythm tighter. She started by licking the underside of his shaft, his swollen balls, before running her tongue all the way up to the tip several times, blowing softly as she went. Lightly covering her teeth with her lips, she let the head of his penis glide into her mouth, licking the spot underneath the ridge of his head and making him shiver. Her tongue never stopped its movement, running back and forth, up and down, side to side, as he got harder and harder until he couldn't imagine there was any blood left anywhere else in his body.

With one hand at the base of his cock, thumb and index finger circling the shaft, pulling the skin back, as he'd showed her, she began to coordinate her tongue strokes with her hand strokes, building up speed and pressure, accelerating her technique in time with the rising speed of his pulse, as everything seemed to move faster and faster and her hand shifted the skin back as though it were fabric, and first his pre-cum leaked out and then, when he thought he was simply going to explode in her mouth—he did, and the white liquid filled her mouth as her lips stayed tight, and she swallowed and he sighed, and then the world fell back into place.

If he'd been able to open his eyes, he would have seen that nothing had really changed, but everything was spinning too fast to allow him to do that, and once she'd collapsed happily next to him, he had no reason to look at the rest of the room. Everything he wanted was on the bed with him.

He reached over to take her hand, and she kissed him.

"Want to play some more after breakfast?" she asked.

Laughing, he said, "It would be my treat."

At The Gate

Somehow I got through check-in faster than I'd expected. I was up, waiting by my gate, a full three hours before take-off. My bags had been inspected, my clothing metal detected, and my seat assigned—all about thirty minutes faster than predicted. To add insult to injury, the flight was delayed by an hour. Even more insulting, the gate had no duty free.

I was left to kill 180 minutes without shopping, without even a café in which to buy food that I would feel guilty for eating but which would still entertain me during those minutes it would take to consume it.

There was nothing to do but wearily turn the pages of my book, which already bored me, and to stare at my fellow passengers, who bored me even more, while waiting for the second hand to make its way slowly around my watch until I could stand up again and relocate my boarding pass.

I turned pages, I stared listlessly, while the second hand crawled. I indulged in an ice cream cone from the vending machine. I bought a sandwich from the man selling them in the corner, off a small folding table which reminded me of children's lemonade stands, while making me wonder if this delay was actually a conspiracy on the part of the airport to collect as much of our change as it could before we fled the country.

Other than those two consumption-fueled trips, I refused to move from my seat, tethered by my laptop to the one seat in the waiting room located in front of an outlet.

I alternated between absentmindedly photoshopping some images I'd been meaning to get to and turning the pages of my book, which was supposed to be a thriller, but I couldn't imagine anything making time move slower than its painstaking pace. When that got boring, I treated myself to a trip to the bathroom. Then back to my seat, back to photoshop, back to the book, and the routine continued.

One hour managed to be lost in such a fashion as I tried to ignore the people gathering behind me in the vestibule, where an informal smoking session had been organized by a group of desperate fellow passengers unable to cope with the prospect of not smoking until their destination, a distant time of release growing all the more elusive as departure time grew more indefinite. The group grew larger, the smoke grew thicker, the conversation more annoying jovial, and then someone leaned up against the wall.

Just then, an alarm went off.

Apparently, one of the smokers had pressed something that should not have been pressed (and would not have been pressed if it hadn't been for the delay and the smoke and the desperate smokers with their desperate conversation), and it was loud.

Piercing, in fact.

I winced but refused to move from my assigned seat. No one else seemed interested in moving, either. We all stood (or sat) and waited for things To Be Taken Care Of.

Apparently, smokers don't often loiter in the vestibule, or, if they do, they don't often lean up against the wall, because no one seemed to know what to do or how to make it stop.

Just when I was contemplating unplugging my laptop and moving, at least, to the other end of the room, to get a bit further away from the wail, it stopped. Everyone collectively exhaled. I, too, sighed with relief and looked up to see if there was anything to see—and there was.

She was about my height, with short brown spiky hair, one diamond stud earring in each ear, brown eyes, and wearing a well-tailored airport security suit that conveyed an element of Dietrich sophistication while still expressing a delicious sense of comfort and control. She was cool and collected, she knew how to turn the alarm off, and I didn't need that suit to be any more snug to imagine what lay underneath.

I was in love. Both with her and the silence she had created.

I was also at the gate of an airport terminal. It wasn't exactly a bar. I couldn't buy her a drink. I couldn't ask her to dance. I couldn't give her my phone number—I was on my way out of the country, after all.

What might have been came together as an MTV montage of soft-focus imagery and rapid-fire editing. If only I'd met her a month earlier, we could have spent four weeks together, at the movies, in the dark, in bed, on the dance-floor, holding hands, holding bodies, touching lips and legs and arms and hands—but now, now it was too late. My timing was never right.

Who meets someone in an airport terminal? How can it have a chance of surviving? The only time you are sitting and waiting in the airport is when you are sitting and waiting to *leave.*

"Excuse me?"

I looked up. It was her. Her. Her. Her. She was talking to *me*. I scrambled to attention, feeling like a young marine caught asleep on duty.

"Uh, yes, yes?"

"Do you mind unplugging your laptop for a second? We just need to use the outlet. It'll just be a minute."

Her tone was civil. Polite. Distant. If she was also fantasizing about ripping off my clothes in the nearest, she wasn't letting on.

"My outlet? Oh, yeah, of course, sure."

I bent down awkwardly, reaching underneath the chair, and pulled. The cord flew out of the wall with perfect precision, but the adaptor, my American to European power adaptor, decided not to be so cooperative and, instead, fell limply into the grate that marked the transition from floor to wall.

"Fuck," I said.

"I'm sorry? What's that? Is everything okay?" She kneeled down to look under the chair, and I tried to keep my balance while her head was inches from my shoulder and the entire world smelled of her perfume.

"My adaptor fell. My power converter, you know? It fell in the grate."

"Oh no," she said.

My knight in an army security suit crouched down even further and tried to yank the grate away from the floor. No luck. She shook it a bit and tried again. Nothing.

I sighed. "That's okay. I lose them all the time."

"No, no. Don't worry. We'll get it out."

Oh god, this was all I needed. My brown-haired beauty, instead of seducing me in an empty hallway, was going to save the day by inconveniencing herself underneath an airport waiting room chair. I couldn't allow that.

"No, really. It's okay. I can buy another one."

I stood up, and she stood up with me. We were standing, face to face, eyes at the exact same height, her brown looking into my blue, and I completely forgot that there was anyone else in the room. I completely forgot about my flight, about the smokers, even about the vestibule. For a minute, my brain started to piece together what I would say when I called my mother to explain that I was not, actually, going to be heading home that day, since I would be staying for another few weeks in order to get to know my new girlfriend properly.

"I've got the perfect idea!"

I blinked. Was she reading my mind? Was she going to propose buying a ticket and coming with me to spend the summer in my parents' dark basement? Was she going to suggest trading in my ticket so we could go to Paris, instead? Or maybe Spain?

"I think we have some adaptors in the main office. Maybe I can just go see and then if we have an extra, I can give it to you? Is that okay? I don't think your plane is boarding for at least another hour."

Oh. The adaptor. I'd forgotten.

"That would be great. Thanks so much." I did my best to smile a 1960s mom smile, the kind that promised deep fudge brownies and ice cream after dinner.

She smiled back.

"I'll be back in a minute," she replied, turning away from me.

No, no, no, no, no. I couldn't allow this. To be so close and yet so far? Never.

I grabbed her arm as she started to walk away.

"Hey, I'll come with you, if that's okay? I'm not doing anything here." I laughed nervously.

"Sure. Come on."

I hurriedly grabbed my bags and my laptop and rushed after her, feeling like a second grader following her teacher to the new classroom location. The only difference being, of course, that as we walked, and I adjusted my bags more properly, as I fastened my laptop into its carrying case, and started feeling a bit more together, I could feel my confidence returning, and, as my spine straightened, I could feel thoughts entering my brain that second graders should never be thinking, least of all about their teachers.

I grinned to myself. I was being a very naughty girl.

We didn't say anything to each other as we walked, virtually in single file, through the labyrinth of airport office hallways, my eyes fixed on the neatness of her uniform, of the perfection of the pleats that brought it in just so at the base of her spine, at the way the legs flared a little at the ankle, accentuating the length of her leg, and the way the pants hugged her ass so tightly, I wondered that it hadn't split when she'd crouched down.

"It's just here," she said, turning to me over her left shoulder as her right hand grabbed the nearest doorknob.

"Great," I replied, peering around her shoulder into the office.

It was the standard office affair, the only exception being that the view out the window was of a huge expanse of runway and the occasional plane. Otherwise, it had the cactus plants on the window, the institutional desk with the institutional computer and the obligatory file cabinets beside the obligatory wall calendar.

"Come on in," she said as she gestured to the extra chair that faced the desk. "Have a seat while I look. It's probably more comfortable than the waiting room!" She laughed and I smiled back at her.

I rested my bags on the floor and sat neatly in the chair, watching her paw through the desk's large drawers.

"I'm pretty sure they're in here, if they're not, maybe they're in the office across the hall, but I'm pretty sure I saw at least one here the other—oh, yes, there it is!"

She raised her hand triumphantly. In her palm was, indeed, an American to European power adaptor.

"Oh, fantastic!" I exclaimed, standing up. I walked over to the desk and reached forward to claim my new replacement adaptor.

Her hand reached forward to my expectant palm and rested it gently, as though it was a precious diamond. While her hand hovered above mine, she looked up at me slowly, and we stared at each other, not moving. Everything was suddenly silent. I looked at her eyes, noticing the flecks of gold in the brown. I saw the way her lower lashes seemed as thick as her upper ones. The lines extending outward from her lips. The smooth line of her nose. The way the light seemed to caress her cheekbones.

I didn't know what to say. I cleared my throat awkwardly. A smile spread across her face, making perfect little wrinkles around her eyes. Her hand was still holding the end of the adaptor that wasn't rested on my palm. I hadn't moved an inch.

"I just realized I never told you my name. I'm Jill."

"I'm Liza."

"Nice to meet you, Liza."

"Nice to meet you, Jill."

We stood, staring. Silence had returned. I was just about to clear my throat again, when she continued.

"And now you've got your new adaptor."

"Yes, now I do."

"What do I get for it?" she asked, grinning at me.

We still hadn't moved. I didn't know what to say.

"What would you like?"

Her face got serious. Her lips reformed into a beautiful Angelina Jolie pout. She stared at my eyes. We held this pose.

"I think you know."

I was about to say I didn't, I was about to say I had no idea, I was about to clear my throat to make some kind of excuse, I was about to stammer an explanation, something pathetic and desperate and awkward—but then I decided not to do any of that, and, instead, I leaned over and kissed her, my hand with the power adaptor clutching her hand tightly, the adaptor pressing into both our palms as my lips pressed against hers. I tasted her mouth as her tongue, so soft, pushed its way into my mouth, and then my other hand came around her waist and shoved her against mine. From her lower back, a line ran directly to my stomach, our thighs squeezed against each other, as if we needed every inch of contact to make this moment feel more real.

Then I slid my hand down her back and across her delicious ass in those pants that didn't leave anything to the imagination and pulled her even closer.

"So what does a girl like me have to do to get inside your clothes?" I whispered in her ear.

"Just unzip," she whispered back.

Oh, the beauty of institutional clothing. One quick gesture removed the jacket, another opened the shirt, while a third sent the pants to the floor.

She was even more stunning with her clothes off. Her limbs were lean and tan and endlessly curving along each perfect hip, thigh, and breast. I stared.

"Come on, you're making me nervous," she said, laughing, crossing her arms in front of her chest.

I shook my head, smiled back at her. "Don't be ridiculous." I spread her arms open and slipped the shirt off. "You're gorgeous."

She grinned at me, a mixture of pleasure and embarrassment. "Can I see you?"

"Of course." Smiling back at her, I pulled my shirt over my head and dropped my jeans on top of her pants.

"You're perfect!" she exclaimed, grabbing me around the waist and pulling me against her.

Our mouths fell into each other again, only this kiss seemed to express a familiarity twice as deep, as though we'd already done this a million times. I sent my fingers across her body, trying to catch up, but it didn't matter how many times I felt her lower back, how many times I touched her breasts or her stomach, how many times my nails raked across her thighs, I always felt like it was still the first time, and I couldn't believe how soft the skin, how smooth she was under my hand.

"Touch me, please," she breathed into my ear. "Please, put yourself inside me…"

I didn't need any further instruction. Ignoring my nagging shyness, I encouraged myself, and my fingers, to get swept up in the energy of the moment, and I slipped them inside her.

She was even softer and smoother there.

"Oh yes, oh yes," she panted, arching herself against my hand, pushing her hips in a one-two fashion onto my wrist, while I pressed up and in, pulled down and out, pressed up and in, pulled down and out. The beat was magic, the rhythm perfect, and all I could feel was the wetness of her insides as they trickled down my hand and the heat of her body, both outside and in.

The more I pressed and pulled, stopping only to flick my index finger across her clitoris, the more she arched and pushed, her hands clawing my back, her mouth threatening to devour mine, her tongue trying to escape her mouth as it shoved its way into mine and I felt like we might somehow, symbiotically, become one.

And then, absurd as it sounds, it felt like the room was lit with a display of white and yellow fireworks and she dissolved onto my hand, the moment feeling fluid as it swept around me in a blur of light and heat and sweat, and she quivered against me, and I pressed her all the closer, enchanted by the sensation of feeling her from the outside and in.

"That was amazing, thank you," she said, her chest heaving in a manner that was somehow both primal and graceful.

Even while I watched her slowly regain her breath, I still wished she wouldn't, because I knew that I was the one responsible, and I couldn't help feeling proud that this formerly immaculate security supervisor's chest was heaving as a reaction to my efforts, and the sentimentalist in me didn't want the moment to stop.

As if sensing my fascination with hers, she ran her finger down my chest, across my stomach, and between my legs.

I'd had no idea how swollen and aching I was until her fingers filled my insides, and it seemed like every inch, every movement, every sensation sent rockets shooting by my ears, sent colors across my retinas, and I felt cut open as though by flares of sensation trailing confetti across the horizon of my insides.

She didn't stop.

With incredible dexterity and almost military precision, she coaxed me to the fastest, most body-consuming orgasm I'd ever experienced, and the sensations left me shivering with pleasure even after her hand had slipped its way gently outside of my body.

We held each other, slightly chilly as the air struck our damp skin.

"Thank you," I said.

She grinned at me, pulling her head back so she could look me in the face. "No, thank *you*."

We both laughed.

"Come on, I should get you back to the gate."

"Oh yeah, right. I forgot."

We both laughed again, a mixture of euphoria and nerves.

Getting dressed, like always, seemed to take more time than getting undressed, but it still didn't take as much time as I would have liked. I didn't want to leave that office, I didn't want to go back to my gate, I didn't want to think about the fact that I was about to leave and would never see her again.

But that moment came, like it always does.

We stood at the door to the office, her hand on the knob, the room silent as we stared at each other.

The air seemed to hang, the moment dragged, as if somehow, the longer we stared, the less we said, the more we could somehow take control of the situation and make reality evaporate into the ether of a bad dream.

But that never works.

So we kissed one more time, looked at each other one more time, and then walked back down the hallway, towards the gate and my fellow passengers.

Only, when we got there, they were gone.

Jill and I looked at each other in shock, with a little bit of fear.

"Have they left?" I asked. "Did I miss my flight?"

Panic set in.

"Don't worry. Stay here. I'll go check."

My knight in an army security suit raced down the stairs and back to the check-in area, while I paced around nervously, staring out the windows and trying to figure out where everyone could have gone and what I was going to tell my mother.

She was back, a moment later, trying in vain to conceal the grin on her face.

"I'm afraid your flight has been postponed until tomorrow, and the airline is responsible for providing your accommodation for tonight. Can I suggest a good hotel?"

I laughed and grabbed her hand.

"Let's go check in."

DAHLIA SCHWEITZER

Late At Night

The light was glowing blue when I peered out from behind the door, clutching the towel around my body. It was dark and incredibly still, the way it feels when everyone has gone to bed, and no one has started waking up. It felt safe to rush across the living room in tiptoe. Even though my slightly-too-small towel an adequate cover, I still preferred not to run into anyone, since it wasn't my house and it wasn't my family, and I didn't want to have to explain why I wanted to take a shower at 3am, anyway.

So imagine how I felt when I realized that the light was glowing blue in the shape of a halo around the head of Jen's older brother, as he sat, typing away on the keyboard.

"Hi there," I whispered nervously, caught in mid-tiptoe, trying to make the towel reach higher at the same time that I tried to pull it lower. "I'm just going to go take a shower."

He glanced up, looking my way but not really seeing me at all. "What? Oh, that's fine. The pressure's not so great, but at least it gets hot."

I smiled. He smiled back, registering eye contact for a minute, before turning his head back to the monitor. With that somewhat formal dismissal, I hurried into the bathroom, hoping that the blue light had concealed the blush which I was sure had spread into bright red circles on both of my cheeks.

Although, to be honest, my cheeks could have gone green, and he probably wouldn't have noticed. I'd been in love with Jack ever since I'd first started hanging out with Jen, when hanging out meant Barbies and choreographing dance routines with the babysitter's help, and my adoration only got worse when the babysitters stayed home and the Barbies were phased out. He'd always been around, but around in the sense that he'd pass the room as we were planning new levels of hide and seek, we'd get a nod or a pat on the head, I'd be left swooning, and that would be that.

When Jen and I got to high school, I considered it a mark of some sort of triumph that we were all finally in the same building together, although the chasm between ninth and twelfth grade was huge enough to render that technicality irrelevant. Occasionally, Jen and I managed to score a ride home from school with Jack, but those lucky moments were few and far between, as no 18-year-old boy wants to drive his sister and her friends around.

If I saw Jack on school grounds, he didn't ignore me, but the passing nod hadn't improved over the years. If I saw him at Jen's house, I'd get a hello, how's-it-going, but he rarely stayed in the room long enough to hear my response. I'd gotten used to it, this silly crush-from-afar-that-would-never-go-anywhere, and I knew that once he left for college, I'd probably never see him again.

C'est la vie.

But I'd forgotten to take into account holidays and summer vacation—which is how we ended up here, one hot August night, with me sleeping over at Jen's, and Jack hunched over his computer, and my feelings evident in the flush of my cheeks and the tingling of my skin and my inability to put more than three words together whenever he was within ear shot.

Even though I was now 18, and my high school years were behind me, I still didn't know what to say to Jack, and I still wanted to rush out of the room every time he came in. At the same time, I wanted to press myself up against the wall, inconspicuous as possible, in order to stare at him, in order to watch the way his hips moved and the shape of his arms under his shirt, in order maybe, just maybe, to have that grin turned,

42

for a few seconds, in my direction.

That rarely ever happened, but it did happen just enough for the visual image to be burned into my retinas for proper repeat viewing, and for the occasional flashback whenever I walked into a room and surprisingly found him there. The grin would blink on my eyelids like a supersonic strobe, and I'd stammer some response before hurrying out of the room.

Which all goes to explain the state I was in as I stood under the shower. The night was so hot and sticky, and the air-conditioning on the fritz, so I'd hardly been able to sleep against the damp sheets. I'd figured maybe a shower would help cool me down, but now, after my unexpected encounter, cooling myself down seemed out of the question, and I felt sure I wouldn't sleep for at least another two days. Something about the way his eyes bore into mine, even if only for a fraction of a second, made me feel like I might never need to sleep again.

As I made my way cautiously out of the bathroom, towel still clenched around me as before, only this time it felt smaller as well as wetter, I saw that Jack was still at the computer. I tried to slip my way across the room on invisible feet, but he stopped me.

"Jen. Hey. Why don't you come look at this?"

I froze in my tracks, pivoting slowly to face him.

"Come, come here," he said, gesturing me over, his eyes still fixed to the screen.

I walked over, feeling like all time might have stopped, or at least as though I was moving through quicksand while my blood seemed to accelerate through my veins.

"Yes?" I asked, trying to keep my voice low and even.

"I'm just finishing this animation for a school project. It's for 3D video game. Can you tell me what you think?"

I peered over his shoulder and watched the little video movements of a car driving through dimly lit streets.

"You see," he said excitedly, "you've got the viewpoint of the car. And you're driving through this town, which is sort of a mix of Prague and maybe someplace in Hungary, sort of dark and mysterious, and you're working for Interpol, and you're looking for these spies that are meeting that day, and you've got to find them—hey, can you see?"

He turned his head around to face me, and our eyes locked. I could barely breathe, with the full force of those blue eyes staring straight, uncensored, into mine.

"Yeah, uh, yeah, I can see," I stammered, feeling incredibly self-conscious and as if, somehow, he could see everything I had always tried to hide.

He laughed. "Come here, come sit around here."

Not exactly sure what was going on, I stumbled around the edge of the chair and somehow sort of collapsed onto his lap just as his legs started to move, the towel still tightly clenched around me, my little fists feeling like those of a baby clutching his mother's finger.

He laughed again. "I didn't exactly mean that, I was going to offer you the chair instead, but this works for me if it's okay for you…?"

I giggled nervously. Oh dear. I couldn't do anything right when he was near. I felt incredibly conscious of how short the towel was and of just how much thigh I was exposing.

I started to get up.

His arms, wrapped around my waist, pulled me back down.

"No. Sit. It's better this way, because you can watch as I do the controls."

"Are you sure I'm not too heavy?" I asked, feeling like a grade school idiot.

He snorted. "You must weigh about twenty pounds. I can take it. Here, let me show you how the game works…"

In a matter of seconds, his explanations about the arrow

keys, and the space bar, the mouse, how to zoom in and zoom out, and how to jump over stairs, faded into a low hum in the background, as all I could feel was his arm around my waist, his legs underneath mine, and his cock slowly getting hard against my ass, naked underneath the towel.

I tried to pretend I didn't notice. I tried to pretend I knew how to levitate. I tried to pretend I was David Copperfield. If I could make my body just a little bit lighter, if I could just lift myself up a fraction of an inch, then I wouldn't feel him underneath me, and he wouldn't feel me feeling him.

The levitation didn't work, but I did manage to press my toes into the carpet, making myself a fraction lighter. It wasn't enough. I could still feel him against me.

At first, I truly thought it was my imagination. His voice didn't change, his patter kept rushing right along, in tandem with the car racing around the streets of Prague (or was it Hungary?), and there was no sign of anything untoward except for the gradually increasing pressure of his cock against my ass—and then I started to realize that I really was naked underneath the towel, and I was starting to get more than a little wet between my legs, and the droplets of liquid didn't have far to go before slipping across my thigh to stain his pants.

I wanted to squirm, but I felt frozen. I couldn't move. If I moved, then he'd know that I knew, and the situation would get ten times more awkward than it already was, and so I just sat there, like a ventriloquist's dummy, nodding my head, willing the wetness to miraculously freeze on my thigh, but knowing I was fighting a losing battle as the drops drip-drip-dripped their way down my naked skin and onto his pants.

I knew I (and the drops) wouldn't stand a chance as soon as his arm (the one that wasn't working the mouse but was wrapped around my waist, instead), seemed to clench my waist a little tighter and then, imperceptibly, pull me back, so that I was against his chest, my head almost on his shoulder, and I could feel his lungs going in and out behind my back, and he stopped talking, so all I could hear was his breathing and the faint hum of the computer.

We sat like that, and I gradually relaxed my neck, my head falling lightly onto his shoulder as I leaned back against him, his left arm still around my waist, while our chests moved slowly in and out, and the night seemed to get darker and more silent, somehow, while I willed the moment never to end.

With a touch so light, I almost didn't know if it was actually happening or was just an event of my imagination, the fingers that had, moments before, manned the arrow keys, were now tracing their way down my neck and across my collarbone.

Despite my shy gratefulness that the steadily shrinking towel managed to cover the basics, every inch of exposed skin was still eagerly awaiting its turn to feel his touch. I couldn't wait him for him to reach my shoulder, to touch my arm, to return to my neck, to remember my thighs. I sat motionless and quiet, the rational sensible part of my brain in a panic, but the arch of my spine, the curve of my shoulders, the openness of my arms was all the declaration I could have hoped to make—touch me more, touch me there, touch me again, touch me even more.

Thank god he wasn't saying anything. If my ears had had to listen to his words, to his voice, I might have exploded from the over-stimulation. As it was, the lower part of my body was willing the fabric between us to disintegrate so that I could feel him inside me, not just against me, and the upper part of my body tingled from his touch, or the anticipation of it, as his fingers traced the lines and curves of my flesh.

Trace those lines, he did—all the way down my arms and onto my thigh and then, before I knew which way to move, his

46

fingers were between my legs, slipping across the wet skin, underneath the towel, and up, up, up, inside. My eyes closed, my back arched, he seemed to fill spaces I didn't know I had with sensations I didn't know I could feel. I don't know if it was two fingers or three, I could barely tell if it was one hand or two—my consciousness only managed to register the fact that he was going in and out, and when he was in, he pressed against the back of my clitoris with an urgency that made me moan, and when he was out, he ran circles around the outside of my clitoris with a lightness and grace that sent shivers down my legs.

And every time I arched or tensed or pressed or moaned, I felt him harder against me, and I desperately wanted to feel him inside me, but I didn't know how to move, and I didn't know if I even could. All I could do was spread my legs and feel my clitoris swelling and beg him to bring me closer and closer to whatever was next.

The amazing thing was that I didn't even really have to move. He slipped his hand between my legs, which were already spread enough to allow him to reach and open his own zipper, and, without any underwear to interfere, his cock was out, glistening in the blue light of the monitor, and then it was inside me.

If I thought it felt amazing before, I'd never have imagined this. I hadn't had a lot of sex in my short-lived post-adolescent romantic career, so I was hardly an expert, but I'd done it with several boys, including John Miner, the star of the soccer team, and it had never felt like this. Even Paul, in the back of his Cadillac, local legend as he was, who'd made me come more than once even though I couldn't stand his conversation, had never left me feeling like this. Jack kept his right hand making light circles on my clitoris while, now, his cock had replaced his fingers, and, as I shifted myself forward just so, and he (with his arm around my waist) held me down, he was all the way inside, deep and hard against me.

Still hesitant, overwhelmed as I was by how it all felt and by the very fact of what was actually taking place, I knew I was fighting a losing battle against the towel. Even though the only light in the room was the blue of the monitor, I still wanted it to get darker. I didn't want him to see me. I didn't want to see him. I didn't want to be more aware of what was happening than I already was. With every passing upward shove of his hips, with every downward shove of mine, the towel seemed to shrink evermore as I struggled to hold onto it, in some pretense of modesty.

"Give me that," he said, voice heavy in my ear. With a dramatic tug, like a magician revealing a bunny, the towel was gone, discarded to the floor, and I was suddenly twice as aware of my breasts bouncing to the rhythm of his knees.

It seemed as though so was he.

The hand that had been latched around my waist slid its way up over my chest, cupping my breasts, as he continued to shove and push his way against me, while every sensation was now compounded by the feeling of his fingers pinching and caressing my nipples.

The speed of the bouncing grew faster, the pressure of his fingers grew tighter, my self-awareness replaced by the rhythm and the force and the in and the out and the arching and the tightening and the pressing back and pushing forward, while he grew faster and I grew wetter, and I couldn't see the blue light of the computer anymore, I couldn't see anything any more, I just heard his breath in my ear and felt his body inside and under me, my thighs were wet and his hot, his cock inside me half the size of my body, bumping and bouncing and shifting and sweating, and then he exploded into me and I disintegrated onto him.

I felt like a painting I'd seen in art class, 'Nude Descending a Staircase,' where everything is split into fragments, and you can't tell where you are supposed to look exactly, and it's like a broken image, but still, somehow the parts make up a whole and you don't even know how you'd combine them to make it more perfect.

"Oh Jesus Christ," he panted in my ear, and I gasped as he heaved and his body bucked under mine, and I felt like I was riding through the rodeo, and Duchamp's painting was kicked out of my head, replaced by flashing images of bulls and matadors and red flags which burst into white brightness, and my hands grabbed his thighs, and my nails dug into his flesh, and I pushed myself down harder onto him and he pressed himself deeper into me.

And then air flooded my lungs as I took a huge deep breath, and he took a huge breath, and we sagged into each other, laughing and weak, and the room was blue again, but my skin was still tingling, and he was inside and around me, and we were both completely wet, and I couldn't tell exactly where his body ended and mine began, and his fingers seemed to belong on my breasts and his cock seemed to belong to my insides, and we just sat there, breathing each other in while the monitor glow flickered.

Slowly, sound came back. First it was the hum of the computer. Then the rustling of our feet on the carpet. I knew the moment was over. The silence had to be broken, but I didn't know what to say. It was as though none of this had ever happened, I still didn't know what to say to him. I still felt like a grade school idiot. Only now I was naked in the blue light and I desperately wished I could grab the towel off the floor and somehow teleport myself to my room. That all this had happened in the safety of a dream.

If only it had been a movie. Or a TV show. We could have cut to the credits and there would have been no awkward post-fuck conversation.

I took a deep breath and leaned over to get the towel and

stand up. He didn't say anything. Oh fuck oh fuck. I wrapped the towel around me and slowly turned to face him. He was staring straight at my face. We looked at each other. Still no words. I had to say something.

And then I knew it. From Duchamp to bulls to Carrie Bradshaw. Another visual image in my brain. I didn't have to say anything at all. If I acted like this was totally normal, he'd think maybe it was. Oh, Carrie, with the high heels and the chirpy voice. I smiled—to myself and to him.

He smiled back at me. It might have been my imagination, but he seemed nervous. Maybe he was wishing he was fully clothed, as well?

I leaned over, kissing him lightly on the mouth. Think Carrie, I thought. Be cool.

"Good night," I said, evenly, my voice conveying every ounce of confidence I didn't feel.

"Good night," he said, sounding relieved.

I turned to walk away, wanting to run my way across the carpet, to my room and my bed where I could relive it all over again.

He stopped me, reaching up to grab my wrist.

"Hey, lady, come back anytime."

My heart a fluttering mess, I smiled down at him, an image of collected cool. Oh, Ms. Sarah Jessica Parker, thanks for the inspiration.

"I will."

And with that, finally, I scampered back to my room, eager to lie in bed and remember every last damn moment.

Like A Virgin

Alexa had wanted to fuck Bill forever, but he was the kind of guy who liked to sleep with girls he chose, not the other way around, so she knew that the only way she'd get him was by pretending the exact opposite of what she really wanted. And since Alexa was a clever girl, she wanted to make it really worth her while.

So Alexa pretended to be a virgin.

She confided in him one night, after the others had gone home, across a table littered with empty pint glasses, the bar mostly empty and dark, leaning across the table, conscious of the way the candlelight would emphasize her wide-open eyes and mascara-ed lashes.

"You've never done it before?" he asked, incredulous.

"No. No, I haven't," she replied, a mix of shy and demure, looking down at her hands, wrapped around her still not empty pint glass.

"How is that possible?" he exclaimed, a little bit drunk, a little bit slurry, his wide-open eyes fixed on her face. "I always kind of figured it happened eventually, even if the girl didn't want it. I mean, you've dated before, right?"

"Oh yes, oh yes, of course." She looked up for emphasis. She certainly didn't want him to think she had 'Mental Issues.' "It's just, oh, I don't know…I guess, the longer you wait, the more you feel like the first time should be right, should be with someone who is good…" (here she left it intentionally vague about whether she meant good in bed or just a good person).

"And then you keep waiting, and it gets to be a bigger deal than it is, and you wonder if you should wait til marriage, since at least that justifies the delay—" she laughed "—but really you just want someone who really wants you and that you really want in return and then you can do it together lots of times and it's not a big deal anymore, it's just fun."

He nodded.

She was having a hard time not laughing, but she just looked back down at her hands, took comfort in his drunkenness and the low light, and waited the appropriate thirty seconds before looking back up.

"I'm sorry, I shouldn't have said anything. I don't really like to talk about it. It's kind of, you know, embarrassing, and uh…"

"Oh, don't worry, I won't tell anyone!" he proclaimed. "Your secret is safe with me." He paused. Reflected. "I appreciate you telling me. Thank you."

She smiled. "You're welcome…and now I should really go home."

Standing up, she leaned over to kiss him goodbye on the cheek. He jumped up.

"Why don't I walk you home?" he offered.

"No, no, that's okay. I'm really just around the corner, so close it's practically upstairs! Why don't you stay to finish your drink, and we'll see each other next time."

He looked at her, looked down at his drink, seemed to think for a minute, and then shook his head. "Let's go." Standing up, he swallowed the rest of his beer in one gulp and smiled at her. "Ready?"

She smiled back at him, grabbed her purse, and led the way out of the bar. She let him walk her to the doorway of her flat, before stopping awkwardly, keys in hand.

"Do you want one more drink?" he asked.

"Oh no, no thanks, I really should go to bed. But thank you."

He leaned over to kiss her and she leaned back to let her

52

lips graze his. She felt his tongue pressing before she darted back, blush on her cheeks.

"Good night," she said, turning into the doorway.

"Good night," he said, staring at her. "Hey, wait, are you around tomorrow? I'll be downtown, and maybe we could have a coffee or something?"

"Sure. Just stop by or call. I should be at home. See you then."

She let the door close behind her before exhaling. She didn't know if she'd succeeded with step one or not, but it certainly seemed like things were going somewhere…

* * *

The buzzer rang at 2 p.m.

"Bill?"

"Yeah, hi, I'm downstairs. Want to come down?"

"Actually, would you mind coming up? I could use a hand with something…"

"What? Oh. Yeah, sure."

She slipped the receiver back in the base while pressing the button to open the door. As soon as she heard the door slam shut, she quickly turned to the mirror and adjusted herself. She was wearing a light blue slip that hung halfway down her thighs. She was wearing underwear but they were very small… She smiled at her reflection as she heard him coming up the stairs.

"Hello," she said, swinging the door open.

"Hel—hello," he said back, blinking as his eyes took her in.

She blushed. "I'm sorry, I'm not dressed yet, I just—I wanted to wear this dress because the weather is suddenly so warm, but it's in this box up there…" She gestured upwards towards a loft space built just under the ceiling. "I've got a ladder but it's old and sort of rickety, and, well, I'm afraid to climb up and get this heavy box and carry it down myself. Would you mind just holding the ladder for me?"

"Oh, of course, no problem. But wouldn't it be easier if I just climbed up myself and you held the ladder for me?"

"I thought of that!" She laughed. "But I've got so many boxes up there, you'll never know which one it is. It's okay. It's not that it's so heavy, it's just that it's tricky because of the weight and the bad ladder. It'll take a minute, and then I'll fix you a coffee. How's that?"

"Sounds fine to me."

They smiled at each other for a couple seconds before she turned to set up the ladder.

"Just hold it here. And here."

With him gripping each side of the ladder, she slipped underneath his arms and made her way up. After about five or six rungs, she leaned forward to sort through the boxes, which, if her calculations were correct, would be leaving him with a view straight up her slip, provided he was looking up. And she felt pretty confident that he was.

She gave him just enough time to get a proper lingering view before turning around.

"I found it," she said, reaching out with a medium-sized box. "Will you just watch me as I bring it down?"

"No problem."

She made her way down the ladder slowly. She had to keep her body further away from the ladder, in order to make room for the box, which left her body closer to his. Which meant that, for a brief moment, as she got to the bottom of the ladder, his arms were around her, as he gripped the ladder, her shoulders and back were against his chest, and she could feel his breath on her neck. She closed her eyes and took a deep breath. All she really wanted to do was to drop the box, spin around, push him up against the wall, tear off his clothes, and ask him to fuck her. But she knew if she did that, she'd never get what she really wanted.

"Whew. That's it," she said, stepping back from the ladder, forcing him to release his hold while she turned, box across her chest. "Just give me a minute to put the dress on…"

"You can stay like that, you know…" he said, grinning at her.

She smiled back. "Come now. You know you wouldn't hear a word I was saying if I did that."

"Is that so bad?" he asked, leaning closer to her.

She just laughed (a little nervously?) and pushed her way past him with the box as her shield.

"One minute, and then I'll make coffee."

* * *

Once safe in her room, she rushed to check her face (ok), her hair (ok), her tiny underwear (after a quick adjustment, also ok), slipped on the dress, and went back to the kitchen.

"Hi."

He turned to look at her. "That's a beautiful dress," he said.

"Thank you."

"Although I still prefer you naked."

She laughed. "How would you know?"

"Good point. Why don't you let me see and then I can be the judge?"

She laughed again. "No chance. I'm not that easy. Coffee?"

"Shame about the easy, yes for the coffee."

He sat at the table and glanced through the newspaper while she filled up the press and set it on the stove. After she sat down, facing him, he looked up, and they both stared at each other in silence.

"So a guy's really never tried to talk his way into your pants?"

He looked at her. She looked at her coffee.

"I'm sorry. I should drop it. I don't know why I just asked that." He shook his head and averted his eyes.

"It's ok. I guess I'm a little self-conscious about it, but not that much. And yes, they've tried, and no, I've never been convinced." She smiled. "The coffee's ready. Milk? Sugar?"

"Both, please."

She felt him watching her as she got up. When she sat down, she didn't sit facing him, but sat at the other seat, at a forty-five degree angle to him, so that their knees were just inches apart and he could get a better view of her cleavage in the low-cut dress.

She knew that, when she sat down, the dress rode up just enough to expose most of her legs.

She pretended not to notice as he pretended not to stare.

He leaned over and, this time, she kissed him. She kissed him like a fifteen-year-old girl behind the stairs after school had let out, full of urgency and awkwardness and desire. He kissed her back as though it was just the beginning of what he really wanted. When she pulled away, he pulled her close, and they kissed again. He ran his hands down her back and over her ass, and she let him feel, she let him touch, just enough so he could get a sense of what he really wanted, and then she pulled back.

"I don't know about this," she said.

"Am I making you uncomfortable?"

"A little, actually. Yes." She tried to look demure. She put her hands in her lap.

"Hey, look at me." He reached his hand under her chin and tilted her head up. "I don't want to make you uncomfortable, not at all."

She nodded.

"But I want you. I want to touch you. I really want to touch you."

She nodded again, trying not to smile—too much.

"If I promise to stop when you tell me, can I touch you? Can we take it like this—" he put his hand on her knee "—and I'll just move my hand up, an inch at a time, and we'll just stop any time you get uncomfortable. Okay?"

She nodded.

He took her right hand in his left and placed it on his knee. "And you'll do the same, okay? You'll move your hand until you feel uncomfortable—"

"Or until you feel uncomfortable!"

"Right." He laughed. "Or until I feel uncomfortable."

"Ok." She felt his knee under her hand. It felt strong. She felt his hand on her knee. She liked the way it felt. She began moving her hand upwards. He began moving his hand upwards. They both looked at each other and grinned, and then, looking back on it, she couldn't say who broke the rules first, it was almost as though they did it together, but suddenly they were both on top of each other, and he was picking her up, and carrying her into the bedroom, and she didn't know if she should keep playing her game or if she should just let it go and let him do what he wanted to do, and what she wanted him to do to her.

But by the time he was on top of her, by the time she was lying down and he was pulling her dress over her head, she knew they were going way too fast and she knew that she didn't want it to be over so quickly because she knew once he was out the door, that was it, and it *would* be over.

She wasn't going to give up so easily.

So she told him to stop. She took her hand and placed it on his chest and told him to stop.

To give him credit, he did. He panted a little bit, but he did sit back, and he did stop. And he looked at her, and he said, "it's okay, we can take it slow."

And she smiled at him, at the sweat on his forehead, at the bulge between his legs, and the intensity of his gaze. She knew what he wanted, and still he asked her if she wanted him to leave.

"Yes, maybe that's the right thing to do."

He nodded, got up, and walked to the door.

"Can I see you again?" he asked.

"Of course. Why don't you call me?"

He smiled. She smiled back, and then he left.

* * *

It was a couple days before he called, and she'd started to wonder if he would, or she'd miscalculated. But call he did, and when he asked what she was doing that night, it was easy enough to mention the movie she'd rented, and easy enough for him to ask if he could stop by.

He brought a bottle of wine. She'd made sure the apartment was dimly lit. She was dressed casual, but casual in a skirt that hung low on her hips, bare feet at the end of long, smooth legs, and a tightly cut tank top.

"You look great."

"Thanks," she said, blushing. "Thanks also for the wine. I'll open it."

She sat him down on the couch in the living room, returning with the opened bottle and two glasses. "I've got a couple movies, actually. I wasn't sure what I'd be in the mood for. We could watch—"

"I've got a better idea. Why don't you sit here," he tapped the couch next to him, "and let's have some wine and talk for a little while?"

"Ok," she replied, sitting down.

They each took a sip of their wine and looked at each

other. He put his glass on the table, and then he put her glass on the table. They looked at each other again, before she leant over and kissed him. She let her tongue run around the outside of his lips, tasting the sweetness of the wine, first outside of his mouth, and then in. She felt his tongue in her mouth, its softness along the edges of her teeth, as she pressed closer to him. This was no fifteen year old after school. This was the kiss of a college cheerleader who'd finally gotten her moment alone with the football captain.

But unlike the college cheerleader, once temperatures had started to skyrocket, she pulled back.

"I'd like to watch a movie," she said.

He gave the tiniest of sighs. "You're the boss," he answered, with a grin. "Would you like more wine?"

She smiled. "Sure. Fill it up."

And then like good little adults, they turned to face the television, to watch their movie, and drink their wine.

For about twenty minutes.

They were each sitting on either end of the (relatively) small couch. She very subtly (after placing her glass back on the table) shifted so that their legs were touching, so that their hips were adjacent. She gave it another minute and then tilted her head onto his shoulder.

She gave that another couple minutes and then she moved her arm over a couple inches, which left it resting on his thigh.

It stayed there just long enough for him to wonder if it had been an accident, and then she widened her fingers, stretching her thumb and her pinky apart, encompassing as much of her thigh as she could cover. And then she relaxed her fingers. Brought them together. Repeat. Slowly. Lightly. Slowly. Lightly.

Then, as if compelled by gravity, her hand started making its way down the inside of his thigh. But this was not a sudden fall. This was gradual, teasing, miniscule millimeter at a time, kind of movement. Until suddenly her hand was resting on a completely different part of his thigh, and now, when she stretched her fingers apart, her pinky was at the seam in the center of his pants, and even the smallest of her fingers could feel the heat coming from inside there.

Her head was still facing the television, as was his, but by tilting her eyes down, she could see the shifting tensions in his pants, and she grinned.

She left her hand there, slowly massaging his thigh, as though oblivious to the actions of her pinky, although, of course, as her hand inched ever slower in that direction (before slipping back down to the innocence of the knee), it became more and more obvious that she knew what she was doing.

And after a while, it was time to move to the next level. Subtlety could only last for so long.

Still, without looking him in the eyes, she slipped off the couch and between his legs. She unzipped his pants and took him in her mouth.

His entire chest rose and fell with the extent of his exhalation, as he slumped down on the couch, leaning his head back, in a state of utter satisfaction and tension.

His cock was in her mouth, and then it was in her hands, and she ran her tongue along his balls, along the shaft, and then slid him back in for more. In and out, pressure from her lips and from her hand combining with the warmth and softness of her mouth, of her tongue...

And then she looked up at him. He looked down at her.

"I'd like to feel you inside me," she said.

"Really?!" he exclaimed, suddenly shifting into straight posture against the back of the couch.

"Yes. At least, I think so."

He smiled at her. "I'll take it slow."

He took her hand and pulls her onto the couch. She sat, a little awkwardly, on his legs. Staring at her intently, he moved his cock between (but not inside) her legs.

She could feel his tip pressing against her opening, and even though she knew that (logically) she should make him wait, make him suffer, prolong it all, she had lost any patience she might have had. She reached her hand between her legs, took hold of him, and pressed him inside her.

"Just do it," she whispered in his ear, "I'll tell you if it's too much."

"I don't want to hurt you."

"It's ok. I want to feel you. Just go slow…"

He began to push himself inside her. She was so wet, there was almost no resistance. She was holding on to the back of the couch with either hand. Both his arms were wrapped around her back, pulling her into him, using his hands to direct her, to control her, to shift her, to allow for the perfect angles, to allow for a tender speed.

As they strike up their rhythm, she begins to ride him, pushing her hips closer to his with every movement, and as he senses her confidence, he begins to pull her closer, as well. He is so deep inside her, she can feel every inch of his penis moving inside her, and he can feel every bit of her tight insides.

She started to moan, and he lost every ounce of self-restraint. He went faster and harder, and she clenched the couch with her fingers, sticking to each other with sweat, the couch creaking beneath them, her moans now mixing with his, as he spasmed inside her, his cum seeping out, and she pressed even harder, and he responded by pulling her close, not by her hips, but with a hand on either side of the curve of her ass, spreading her even more open, so that each downward thrust pulled on her clitoris, and then, as soon as he put a finger between her legs, rubbing light circles on her clit, it was all over for both of them.

The two of them sighed and collapsed against each other,

chests heaving, the sweat damp beneath them.

"Oh my god," was all she could say.

"Was that okay?" he asked, breathless, and a little nervous.

"Okay? That was amazing." She leaned back and grinned at him. "That was definitely worth the wait."

Novelty

She heard the doorbell ring but there was no movement from the bedroom.

"Mom, are you going to get it?" she called, irritated.

"I'm on the phone. Can you? Tell him I'll be there in a second."

Laura sighed as walked over to the door, grabbing it just as the bell rang a second time. How annoying, she thought, looking at the source of the aggressive ringing. Tall, Arabic, with dark hair flecked with just the tinges of gray, deep brown eyes, tan skin. His looks almost made up for his impatience, she thought, smiling, momentarily distracted from her irritation.

"Oh sorry, I didn't hear anyone coming."

"No problem. It's fine. My mother's slow. Come in, she'll be out in a minute." She was still smiling. Her mother never had men over that looked like *this.*

He stepped past her as she stood near the threshold, one hand on the doorknob, and the entranceway suddenly seemed especially narrow.

"Make yourself comfortable," she said, gesturing towards the couch.

Still standing by the door, she watched him arrange his various belongings. He was different than most of the people her mother had over. He certainly didn't look like a PhD. He definitely didn't look like a writer. In fact, he kind of looked like someone she'd want to meet in a bar. She even caught herself watching the way the muscles of his upper arms showed through the thin fabric of his button-down shirt.

"Can I get you something to drink?"

He looked up, smiled at her, and shook his head. "I'm alright, thanks."

Cute, very cute, she thought to herself, heading back to her room, the grin still on her face—both at his appearance and the novelty of feeling that way about one of her mother's colleagues.

Dictionaries were opened, laptops booted up, papers rifled through, the meeting began—and all other matters disregarded. She could hear their conversation from her room, but nothing about their dialogue stood out. At least that part was like every other meeting. She listened for a little while, curious to hear if he had anything interesting to say. He didn't. It settled into background hum.

"Did you bring the original translation?"

"Yes, of course."

"I'm curious to see how they translated this part...This part here, do you see it? There isn't really the right word in German. I'm not sure..."

"Oh, yes, that. Funny how English seems to have ten words for every one of German. Um, let me look, one second, oh, I see."

"Alright. That takes care of page five. What do you have for the last monologue on page ten?"

"Can you pass the dictionary?"

Blah blah blah. Boring, she thought, turning on her music and closing the door.

* * *

Even though she wasn't listening anymore, nothing changed in the dialogue, and the conversation continued along the same lines, the afternoon began to pass as it always does, until they both took a short pause for refills on the tea, and he excused himself to go to the bathroom.

Only in his haste to open the door, he forgot to knock, and as the door swung open, and the steam slipped out into the hallway, in the split second before he could say sorry and slam the door shut, he saw her, in the water, on her back, every inch of her body shimmering in the heat, her breasts hanging just below the surface with nipples the softest shade of pink he'd ever seen, face glistening, pink lips a slightly darker shade than her nipples, and a perfect brown triangle underneath her stomach.

He stumbled back into the living room, hand damp from sweat or condensation (or both?), to continue the meeting until the bathroom would once again be free, but that plan didn't work so well. He couldn't get her out of his head. That split second was burned into his retinas—the coral pink of the nipples, the alabaster white of the skin, the firmness of the thighs, the length of the legs, the beauty of the lips, the size of the breasts, the softness of the hair…

Nothing mother could say could distract him from thoughts of her daughter. Nothing he did could get that picture out of his head. No debate over word definition, no reference on his laptop, no referral to the paperwork—nothing worked.

And then, when she came into the room, wrapped in only a towel, water dripping, to tell him, with a small grin, that the bathroom was now free—then he felt like he might have lost every ounce of safety and responsibility that adulthood had pretended to give him.

He got up to move towards the now safely vacant restroom, shaking his head as if that might help dislodge his foolish fantasies—this girl was too young for him, he was too old for her, he was there for business with her mother, what kind of dirty pervert was he—only, along the way, as he turned the curve between living room and hallway, he froze, mid-head shake. He blinked. It was as though he'd accidentally stumbled on one of those late night hotel porn channels. The only thing missing was the soundtrack. It was as though the image he'd been trying to excise from his brain had returned in typical Hollywood sequel form—bigger, louder, and much more intense.

He couldn't help staring. No man could have helped staring.

Through the crack in the doorway, in that precious inch or two of space between doorframe and door, in a miniscule window that still managed to reveal enough thanks to an alignment worthy of a choreographer's precision, he saw her, again. Her saw her, naked, again. Only this time there was no steam to obscure detail, to soften the lines of her back, which faced him, or her long legs, the perfect smooth curve of the base of her spine, as she bent over. He watched her rubbing lotion down the front of her thighs, and then the side of her thighs, and then over the round ball of her ass, across her hips and up her waist, while he stood, frozen.

As her hand stroked and rubbed its way up, as her posture straightened, he felt the increasing urge to MOVE MOVE MOVE, but he couldn't. He couldn't tear his eyes away from her youthful figure, from the fall of her blonde hair, from the way the freshly-lotioned skin glistened in the light, from the length of those legs, from the perfection of that back. He felt himself leaning forward, he felt his body aching to step just step closer, one inch closer, to touching. He had to touch that skin. He had to taste that skin. He had to lick and kiss and consume that skin—

But then, as the path of the lotion reached her neck, she turned, and caught his eye.

In that brief second of awkward humiliation, as the flush of embarrassment filled his cheeks and the need for movement and action filled his body, he rushed to the refuge of the restroom, hoping by some miracle that he'd managed to move before her eyes had reached the crack of the door.

He couldn't help but wonder, behind the safety of the door, if, maybe she'd winked at him? If there had been a hint of a grin across her face? But that couldn't be. That wasn't possible. And even if she had, how would he have been able to notice when all his eyes could see, in that teeny tiny second of time after she had turned around and before he ran to the bathroom, was, again, the perfect triangle of hair between her legs?

Shaking his head, he pushed the indecent, inappropriate thoughts out of his mind. He was here for business. He was here for business with her *mother*. He was not here to find a date, to pick up a girl, or to fantasize about the color of her hair, the way it floated on the water and clung damply along her long neck and framed her perfect forehead. The blue of her eyes, the white creaminess of her skin, the pink of her lips, of her nipples, of her cheeks...oh god, it was useless. He stared at his reflection in the mirror as he washed his hands. What kind of fucked up pedophile was he?

Ok, ok, so she was probably around twenty-one or twenty-two. It wasn't like she was twelve. But still—it was completely inappropriate, and he knew it.

Yet, he couldn't remember the last time he felt so alive, so on fire, he couldn't remember the last time his dick felt so hard in his pants, or the last girl whose touch he craved with such intensity.

But this would not do. It would not do at all.

He took a deep breath and exhaled slowly, counting to ten as he dried his hands on the white towel. One more deep breath, he thought to himself, as he adjusted himself in his pants, wincing slightly, a good deep breath could cure anything. To his relief and disappointment, as he walked back down that hallway, her door was now closed, and there were no additional mishaps on the way back to the couch, except for the movie that was now playing in his head, in rapid, pornographic detail.

Back to work. They finished reviewing through page twenty and began the next chapter. He tried to lose himself in the work, to distract himself with the complexities of the German language, to focus on the intricacies of the text, willing her image out of his brain. And he almost succeeded. He managed only to think of her at the end of every other sentence. He managed to forget the way her nipples poked through the water, floating like soft pink islands, until he got to a period, a closing punctuation, and then, with a slight sigh, he'd allow himself one quick visual respite before forging ahead.

Mother, of course, was all business and all tea and he began to think, maybe, just maybe, he'd be able to leave like none of this had ever happened—only, just as he was at the door, just as they were planning their next appointment and recapping what each would email the other, just as his hand was on the doorknob, *her* voice called out, and he flushed, as though he'd done something wrong.

"Hey, would you hold the elevator? I'm heading down, too... I'll be there in a second."

He couldn't tell which emotion hit faster—the panic or the thrill. He tried not to think, he couldn't think, so he just stammered yes as he made the necessary goodbyes. Part of him wished desperately that the elevator would arrive and that, like in all the suspense movies, he'd get inside, and the doors would close just as she came running, and then he'd be able to get away.

The other part of him ran his tongue over the surface of his teeth, hoping there was nothing caught there, adjusted his shirt, checked that his zipper was closed, took a deep breath, and felt each second tick by as he waited to see her again. He couldn't remember the last time a girl had made him feel so nervous and so *young*.

The romantic comedies won out over the suspense dramas, and the elevator doors slid open just as she slipped out of the apartment, grinning at him. He grinned back.

"Are you gonna hold the doors for me?" she asked, smiling, walking towards him.

"Of course," he replied, suddenly feeling ten feet tall. His hand extended to keep the doors open as she brushed past him, and then he stepped inside.

Before he'd really expected it, they were alone together. Alone together in a small metallic box built for four, which meant it was already a little small for two. They played the eye contact game of staring at each other, while trying to look away at the same time, as the elevator hummed them downwards.

"You saw me, didn't you?" she asked, looking coyly up at him.

"What do you mean?" He felt nervous again. His palms were sweating. He put his hands in his pockets, not sure what else to do with them.

"Well, by my count, you saw me twice. Once in the tub, before you closed the door, and the second time, you sneaked a look when I was in my room...didn't you?"

He denied it. She just kept grinning.

"I can tell you're lying."

"Oh yeah?" He couldn't help but grin back at her.

"Oh yeah."

"How can you tell?"

"You're blushing."

With that declaration, as if on cue, the elevator doors majestically opened, and she stepped out. He followed her, starting to make his goodbyes.

"But aren't you going to walk me to my car?" she asked, innocently, only the glimmer in her eyes suggesting the possibility that maybe there was more on her mind.

He had no choice to say yes. He had no choice as a gentleman, and no choice as a man. He knew he should just turn around and walk away, but he couldn't. It wouldn't be right. It didn't feel right. So, together, they walked over to her Acura.

With the key in the door, she turned back to look at him. It was the stereotypical date moment as he stood there awkwardly, not knowing if he should chastely kiss her goodbye on the cheek, if he should lean over and kiss her the way he really wanted to but knew he shouldn't, or if he should politely and asexually nod, before walking away like every other boy that wimped out from crossing that line.

She smiled at him. He smiled back. Something in the air smelled delicious. He wondered if it was her perfume or her shampoo. It smelled sort of like cinnamon and vanilla, and it made him want to get in bed with her and press his head against her shoulder and hold her naked body against his.

"I have a confession to make," she said.

"Really?"

"I left the door open on purpose."

"You left which door open on purpose?" He felt like this might be a test.

She smiled again, glancing down at the ground, peering up at him through those long eyelashes. His stomach flipped.

"You left the door to your room open just a little because you knew I'd be walking by to go to the bathroom?" He cringed as he heard the words coming out of his mouth. Was he really as big an idiot as he sounded?

"Maybe."

She smiled even more broadly, looking especially pleased with herself. He'd figured it out, but he still had no idea how to react. He didn't know if he should be upset (because she was fucking with him) or if he should be pleased (because she was fucking with him). She just smirked as she leaned over, whispering in his ear, "Did it turn you on?"

"Of course it did," he whispered back, acutely aware of how close her lips were to his ear, of how close her body was to his, how warm her breath was on his skin, and how much he really did like the smell of that vanilla.

"Good," she said, opening the car door, and slipping inside. She looked up at him through the open window. "Here's my number." She handed him her card. "Will you call me tomorrow?"

He took the card dumbly, holding it in his hands as though he'd never seen one before. He didn't know quite what to say, he felt like nothing he said would be quite right, so he just nodded, standing there, as she drove off.

* * *

He wasn't going to call her. Really. It didn't take a PhD to figure out she had bad news written all over her, and not only because of who her mother was. Not only because he was too old for her. And not only because he didn't know what he would do with her if given the chance (although he knew—because he couldn't get them out of his head—all the things he imagined doing).

Mostly because she made him feel out of control.

He didn't need to feel like that again. Wasn't there something to be said for security? For routine and comfort? For keeping it simple? What did he need with complications? Hadn't he moved beyond feeling this way?

And yet he called her.

He couldn't help it. He couldn't get the damn girl out of his mind. He called her the next day and said he wanted to meet. She said she wanted to, too, and so plans were made.

It was as easy as that.

* * *

They had Thai food, although it might as well have been Indian for the amount of attention he paid to it). They went to a movie which he barely noticed, because he was so busy staring at her hands, sitting neatly folded in her lap, and waging an eternal battle between wanting to touch them and not being able to bring himself to do it. They had a couple drinks, which only made him feel more desperate and less in control. He asked her if she wanted to go anywhere else. She said no, shaking her head and smiling sweetly, asking him to take her home.

Feeling the sinking feeling of her failure as he steered his car back to her building, wondering what to say as he pulled up in front, feeling like an idiot for having even attempted this kind of thing, he turned to her, words evading his lips, but before the moment could grow awkward, she was kissing him. Her lips, tender, soft, sweet, pushing on his, tongue between his teeth, his head spinning, while he grabbed her to him, feeling her body against his, tasting her in his mouth, her skin beneath his hands. He couldn't believe how much more of her skin he wanted to touch.

And then it was her hand between his legs, her hand on his cock that was pressing tightly against the fabric of his pants, her hand slowly rubbing.

"You can't, we can't, not here," he panted, trying to push her hand away.

She resisted, grinning up at him.

""When I've had a few drinks, I get a little naughty."

He smiled back. "We can't do it here, though. Anyone could see!"

"So?" Her hand was still rubbing back and forth, back and forth, and he was having a hard time distracting himself from the line her shirt was making against her breasts or the rush of blood between his legs.

"Well, can't we go somewhere?"

"You want to come upstairs?" she asked, leaning over, and then, whispering in his ear—"But my mother might hear us…"

He moaned—and not just because of that discouraging fact. The pressure of her hand on his cock wasn't letting up, and he was aching against his pants. He could feel himself already starting to leak a bit, and he didn't know if he had the self control to just drive away, without her. He desperately wanted to go upstairs, to see her, naked, on her bed, beneath him, to feel himself inside her, to be inside her mouth, her body, or even just between her hands.

But her mother. Her mother was up there. Oh god, what was he supposed to do?

"What are we supposed to do?" he asked, turning to her, as her hand's pressure intensified, and he felt any control he might have over the situation slipping away.

She leaned over to whisper in his ear again. "We're not supposed to do anything. We can just do whatever we want…" She ran a finger down his shirt, across his chest and stomach, reaching the top of his pants. With a quick gesture that was over before he'd even realized it had begun, his pants were unzipped, and her hand was making its way beneath his underwear. "What do *you* want to do…?"

He realized his left hand was gripping the door, and the right hand was on the parking brake. He tried to release them, to shift back in the seat, but, just as he did, her fingers reached his cock, wrapped themselves around it, pulling it out from behind the confines of the elastic fabric. All he could do was grip tighter.

"I want to go upstairs," she said. "Won't you come with me?"

With a lingering stroke between his legs, she turned,

opened the car door, and slowly got out. Closing the door firmly behind her, she stared at him through the window.

"Aren't you coming?" she asked.

He shook his head, but it was more to tell himself to stop it, to stop being a baby, because he knew what he was doing. He wasn't saying no. He was following her wherever she led him.

Getting out of the car in a daze, feebly shoving himself back into his pants, he came around to her side, where she grabbed his hand and led the way into the building. As soon as the elevator doors slid shut behind them, she fell against him, pressing him against the mirror, and they kissed intensely during the all too short ride up to the third floor, her pelvis shoved against his, his cock aching to get back out, to get inside her, her lips against his, her hands making their up his shirt, fingernails across his back.

And then they were there.

The doors opened, and she pulled him behind her down the hallway to the apartment, tiptoeing through the living room like a couple of guilty schoolchildren, and into her room. The same room into which, only the day before, he'd spied so illicitly, and now he was there, and now he was being pushed on the bed, and now he was grabbing her down on top of him, and wrapping his arms around her, and pulling off her clothes as she tugged at his, and then they were naked, and then he was inside her, slipping so smoothly through her wetness it was as though there were no friction whatsoever, and it was just the perfect sensation of skin against skin, and the heat of her body made him want to push himself inside as far as he possibly could before pulling out to do it all over again.

It took everything he had not to moan, not to make a sound, knowing that just down the hall, like every teenager's worst fear, was a daughter's mother who could do a lot worse than ground him, but he would willingly have sacrificed, have suffered the indignity of muteness, just to keep feeling himself inside her, her teeth on his nipples, the way his skin tingled at her lingering touches, the sweetness of her breasts in his mouth, her tongue on his, her tongue across his shoulder, his tongue on her neck, his teeth biting her, his fingers in her mouth, and, through it all, his cock pushing in, deeper, pulling out, pushing in, pulling out pushing in, while her legs wrapped around his waist, pressing her even closer to him.

She trembled as he drove himself inside her, kissing her lips, neck, the perfect curve of her ears. He knew she was too young for him, he knew that he shouldn't be allowed the pleasure of skin so tight, so firm, so perfect, but that just made him devour it all the more. The absolute silence which they maintained gave their physicality another dimension, a richness as the other sensations became more acute in the hushed darkness of the room.

He could see her face in the glow from the streetlights, between the silhouettes of the neighboring buildings, her closed eyes, the upturn of her nose, the smoothness of her shoulders and her open lips, and he had to stifle a moan as he buried his head against her neck. He knew he should be old enough to know better, he knew that she could turn his life upside down, but he had to admit to himself that he liked that. It might even have been part of the attraction. He liked knowing his life was still capable of being turned upside down. It turned him on. It made him feel alive again.

Her legs, her long, slender legs, around him, as her knees dug into his waist, her pelvis constricting rhythmically against him, her open mouth inhaling and exhaling in tandem. He could smell the cinnamon and vanilla mingling with the scent of her body and her heat, and his senses could no longer tell where each came started or began (her skin? her hair? between her legs?), but it didn't matter. It didn't matter where anything started or began, because all he could feel, at that moment, was her body around his and the beginnings of his orgasm, rising from his toes, up his legs, as her orgasm sent her clit and her pussy quivering around his cock.

Biting his lip to keep his mouth shut, to keep himself from making a sound, holding her close, as though that would enforce their silence, the two of them came together in a big quiet shudder of sweat and cum and breath, every moment amplified by their quiet, marked by the increasing shallowness of their breath, the growing speed of the inhales and exhales, faster, faster, panting, panting—and then the sudden pause, no breath, no noise, and then the inevitable exhale. The long exhale, followed by another silence, before breathing returned again, beginning to approach normal speed, the inhales and exhales setting the soundtrack as bodies relaxed and disentangled.

"Hey," she whispered.

He turned to look at her. "Yeah?" he whispered back, feeling furtive under the covers, remembering those nights he used to read under the blankets with a flashlight.

"You know you can't sleep here, right?"

He grinned. "Yeah. I know."

"I'm sorry, but you know, it wouldn't be good..."

"It's totally okay, as long as I get to see you again."

She smiled broadly back at him. "Of course you can."

"Maybe you can come to my house next time?" he asked, feeling almost timid with the request.

"Can we make noise there?"

"For sure!"

"Then it's a date."

He laughed. "But will it be as much fun if we're not sneaking around...?"

She giggled, wrapping her arms around him. "We'll figure out other ways to make it fun. I promise."

Online

Clickety-clack…the synchronized sound of many tiny tapping keys as a room full of cubicles echoed with the collective din of Internet correspondence…Clickety, clack. Pause. Space bar. Return. Clack. A wall of white noise fading into the background, blending into the occasional conversation or the occasional telephone call, all of us typing away just a little bit faster as the little time clock of our remaining credit wound its way down.

All of us typing as I shifted in my seat to read my email. The usual correspondence from people who type too much and say too little, but then the best letter of them all…the one I saved for the end, because I knew I'd be useless after reading it.

From: Victor
Date: Sep 23, 2005 7:02 PM
Subject: When You Get Home
To: Lena

Just the subject made me tingle…it made me cross and uncross my legs in anticipation, until, finally, when all the other dreck had been sorted through, when I'd flexed my online banking muscle, when I'd written my mother, and replied to my boss, then, only then, did I double click.

Ah, Vic, the things you do to me with the simple rendition of words on a page.

Hey sweet girl. It's only been a few days, but already I keep checking the date to see how much longer I have to wait until you're back.

*The bed seems larger without you. The nights longer.
Dinner anticlimactic. Bedtime is a waste of time.*

*I want to wrap myself around you and feel you
underneath me. I want to slip myself inside you. I want to
touch your breasts and lick your skin. When can I taste you
again? When can I feel you tasting me?*

I could feel myself blushing as I read his letter, and I
glanced back and forth to make sure no one was watching. No
one was. No one cared. Everyone was typing clickety-clack
while their counters ran on and their credit ran down. No one
saw the blush on my cheeks or my hand surreptitiously make
its down inside my pants and between my legs.

Victor and I weren't really an item, at least not in the
let's-pick-up-dry-cleaning-together way, but we'd started to
date shortly before I left town, and we'd had a couple fantastic
nights together. Being a writer, and a musician, and obviously
therefore a romantic, he was great with words, and wow, could
he write me letters. I loved every one.

I kept reading., my hand between my legs, comfortable in
the fact that I'd put more than enough cash on my credit to last
me well into a couple more internet sessions, I soon forgot I
was even in a public place, losing myself in Victor's words,
his descriptions, and the embellishments my own fantasies
provided.

*...I'm alone (and I truly am) in my single light lit office.
It's late on a Thursday, and staring at this computer is hurting
my eyes and back. My phone rings, and I wonder if it's you. If
you're back. If you never left. It is. I let you in, but I'm
distracted. I sort of ignore you, work still tangling my head. I
sit down and begin to trudge my way through comps, but
slowly your arms wrap around my neck and you press your*

soft hair and cool cheek against my neck and shoulder. You breathe in as you pull me closer and kiss my shoulder tops and nape of neck. You start to rub slowly and ever so gently my shoulders, but soon you press harder up against my chair and back and finally twist me around to reveal a slightly undone top and black bra peeking from its edges.

Oh god, oh god, oh dear…my finger making rapid circles around my cunt, my cheeks hot and burning, leaning forward in the cubicle, trying to hide, riveted by the screen…

You push my face into your chest and I begin to kiss lightly around the edges of the bra and your soft pale skin. I kiss your neck and into the back of your ears and across your jaw to your barely parted lips. I kiss with warmth and you let me in. I pull you tightly against me as you give in to the heat and softness of the wet kiss. Your hips push forward against mine and send a wave up me and I press back and into you, pushing up. My hand winds thru your hair and pulls your head back.

My god, Victor, when did you learn to write like this? Where is this coming from? We haven't known each other for that long, and our sex, in person, has never been so hot…we'd only even had it a couple times. I'd never realized you felt like this, I never realized I felt like this, I never realized I could feel like this…and it's just words, on a screen…

My cunt is beginning to throb, my clit beginning to swell, and I feel like I have mastered the art of the angle, my wrist somehow curved just so, my hand inside my pants but in such a way that I haven't had to unzip anything, shoulder leaning against the wall of my cubicle, eyes half-closed, as I am only half-here…just here enough to hold onto the words, to follow the safety rail of his sentences, and the other half of me lost somewhere over the cliff, floating on air, on sensation, on vibration. Circle after circle, word after word, the combination of my memories of Victor intermingling with his fantasy and my own...

The other hand splays out across your back and holds you solidly on its own, slowly moving your hips and ass into and away from me. Your hands gently slide down to my crotch and one begins to explore and feel me. I moan. You want to drop on your knees and take me but we kiss wetter and softer yet engulfing each other. We breathe quickly and—

"Hi."

I blink.

"What's going on?"

I blink again. What's this? The little text message bubble has popped up in the middle of my screen, interrupting my reading, my fingering, my everything. Blink blink. Mocking my indecision. Blink blink. Without pause, without hesitation. Blink Blink. Bringing me emphatically back from there to here.

I have a message from CRX21. Who the hell is CRX21?

"Who is this?" I type, my right fingers sadly repurposed.

"I can see you," came the rapid response.

Like a student caught cheating, I whirled my head around guiltily, scanning the downward-turned heads of my colleagues. No one looking, everyone typing. I am confused. Clickety-clack.

Blink blink. The message waited for a response.

"Where are you?"

"Nearby."

Blink blink.

I look around again but can't tell which of the many people in the room might be spying on me.

"Who are you?" I ask again.

"What's going on?" came the reply.

"Who are you?" I ask a third time.

"Sorry. Bad manners. Chris. AKA CRX. Ha."

"Are you in the room with me?"

"YES. *Grin.*"

I glance over my shoulders, but I'm just wasting my time. If he's in the room with me, he's not giving himself up so easily.

"What are you doing?"

"I'm reading my mail," I answer, feeling defensive. "What are you doing?"

"Watching you. ;)"

I can feel my cheeks turning bright red. I squirm in my seat.

"For how long?"

"Long enough…"

My god. I am so embarrassed. I creep further in, inside my cubicle.

"Don't worry, I won't tell."

"You won't tell what?" I ask. Who is this guy anyway?

"What I saw…"

I can't help but grin a bit. I like a good game, and I certainly like a good banter.

"What did you see?"

Pause.

Pause.

"I saw you."

Blink blink.

Followed by—

"You, looking hot."

Followed by—

"You, looking very hot."

Followed by—

";)"

I watch the wink blink on my screen.

Blink blink. Clickety-clack.

"What were you reading…?"

For the millionth time, I scan the room, but no one seems to be paying me any sort of special attention.

"I was reading an email."

"From your boyfriend…?"

"No. Just a guy."

"A guy from here?"

"No. Back home."

Who is he? Who is this Chris?

"Why do you care?" I ask him. "Why are you writing to me?"

"Because you're hot. Because I got tired of just watching you and I wanted to talk to you."

"Fine. Then talk to me. Come over here and talk to me."

Pause.

"No."

"Why not?"

"This is more fun."

"Why? I want to know who you are."

"I know. That's why it's fun…"

"Oh come on, let me see who you are."

"No."

Pause.

"Maybe later."

Pause.

"Maybe."

I smiled. This guy was too much.

"So tell me about the letter…"

Ha. The nerve.

"No. That's private."

"Awwww, come on…it must have been hot…I want to

know what you were reading…"

"No."

Pause.

"I can be stubborn, too," I type, laughing out loud. This was fun.

Pause. Pause. Pause.

"Okay. Then I'll write you my own letter."

This time it was my turn to stare at the screen.

"Uh, okay."

The screen was silent for about half a minute during which I stared and squirmed and wondered if I should leave or get a cigarette. And then—

"Even though I couldn't take my eyes off your hand, down in your pants, it's really your mouth I have been thinking about…and how soft it must be and how much I'd love to steal a kiss…to straddle you in your chair and press those delicate lips softly against mine."

Blink blink. I knew it was just my imagination, but it seemed as though the blinking had suddenly gotten brighter. I clicked on the message, but I didn't know what to type in response. Before I could think of what to say, I got another message.

"To feel how wet and smooth and perfect it is when I kiss you. And to continue to slide my hand slowly down your neck and up the back of your head through your hair and pull softly. And then still feeling every inch of your lips pressed fully against mine run my hand down slowly across your chest and start to kiss down your neck......"

Blinking getting brighter. Room getting quieter. My cheeks getting hotter. What the hell was going on? What was I supposed to do? Was this some crazy stalker freak? Who was this? What should I say? What should I type? I knew I should just log out, I should just X my way out of the screen, close the boxes, end the blinking, grab my coat, and leave, leave,

leave.

I could already taste the cigarette in my mouth, could feel the winter air in my lungs. Go, go, go, I thought. Fifteen seconds and you'll be out on the street. Fifteen seconds and you'll be away from this computer, on your way home, on your way out, on your way somewhere, anywhere, out out out…

But I couldn't go.

I couldn't stop staring at the blinking. Sucked in. Seduced. Hypnotized. CRX21, what have you done to me?

Was it his audacity that turned me on? Was it just my compulsive curiosity to discover who he was? Was it just the fun novelty of the whole situation? Was it his very interest in me that made me interested in him? Or did I just want to know what the fuck he looked like?

"I know you're still there."

Yeah, no shit, I'm still here. You spy. I just don't know what to say. My fingers lingered hesitantly over the keyboard.

"Did I scare you?"

"No," I typed without a second's hesitation. "Well, maybe a little."

Pause.

"Sorry. :("

My turn to pause.

"It's okay."

":)"

I laughed.

"What do you want to do to me?"

Okay, now that was taking it too far. "I don't even know what you look like. I have no idea what to do with you."

"Oh. Right. That's okay."

Pause.

"Want to go on a date?"

I laughed. "I don't know. I don't know you."

":) But you will!"

"Oh yeah? Are you asking me out?"

"I imagine it like this. Warm spring afternoon. Long lunch. Meeting in the park for sun and food. You are wearing the top you've got on now, but with a short skirt. I'm wearing what I'm wearing now (ha ha, but you don't know what that is!)…"

Okay, this guy was at least amusing me, crazy stalker freakshow or not.

"We wander up into a hill and woody area. There's no one around. No one to watch. I turn and grab you. Run my hands down your waist and over your ass and I pull you close. You're wearing a pair of white silky (expensive—I bought them for you) hi cut underwear and feeling them beneath my grasp makes me pull your mouth, already wet and warm tighter to me…"

Pause.

"Am I good?" he asks. "Am I as good as what you were reading before?"

I smile. "Yes, Chris, you're good."

":)"

"The kiss elevates from casual greeting to I miss you and need you and want you. We sit, you straddle me. We grind slowly and unnoticeably, even though there is still no one passing by. I'm totally aroused and feel you wet and warm beneath the skirt. Our kisses are heated and begin to stroll across face and chin and neck and shoulder. Our breath is quick and hot and your eyes close and the world, like it does with us, doesn't exist. Faster we move and wetter we kiss…"

My god. I haven't even realized I'm leaking all over myself until the messages stop coming, and the last sentence blinks mockingly on the screen. I've been lost completely in the rhythm of his text, sucked in by the speed of his typing and the imagery of his description—until now, suddenly, I'm not sure what to do.

I stare at the blinking box on my screen. I wonder where he is sitting. What he is thinking. What he will do next. What I will do next.

"Do you smoke?"

"Yes."

"Shall we, then?"

I freeze in my seat. Part of me wants to hide, but I know that's a waste of time. He knows me. He knows who I am. He knows where I'm sitting and what I am doing. I can't exactly hide. There's nowhere for me to go. If I leave, he can follow. If I stay, he can just come over to my cubicle. He's got me. And as long as I don't wander down a deserted street, I've got nothing to lose. Staying in my seat won't get me anywhere, and, honestly, I'm damn curious to know what he looks like. I'm even mildly curious to know how old he is.

"Alright."

I log out of my computer, grab my things, and slowly stand up. I glance around the room to see who is heading in my direction.

No one.

Feeling slightly disappointed, I decide to comply with the instructions, anyway, and I make my way to the door. As I pass by the front desk, I nod at the boy behind the counter.

"I logged out, but I'll be right back, I'm just going to have a cigarette."

"No problem, I'll join you." He winked at me.

I stared.

He came out from behind the desk and reached his right hand forward to shake mine.

"I'm Chris, nice to meet you."

I stared some more, conscious of his fingers grasping mine, the feel of his skin against mine, the warmth of his flesh and firmness of his grip.

He leaned forward and said, gently, with a smile, "I don't know your name."

Somewhere, between the realization of the beautiful blue of his eyes and the startling sweetness of his face, I brought myself back to reality, blush returning to my cheeks.

"Oh, sorry, Lena. I'm Lena."

"I like your coat."

I glanced down. If I hadn't looked, I probably would have forgotten I was wearing anything, I felt so naked in front of him.

"Oh, thank you."

"Shall we?" He reached ahead and opened the door, holding it for me, waiting for me to walk by him, along the length of his arm, and outside to the bracing refreshment of cold air.

I stood on the corner, nervous, at a loss for words, but unable to stop sneaking glimpses at CRX21. He was really cute. I couldn't believe I'd never noticed him properly before. Something about the lighting in an internet café (terrible fluorescent) and the general attitude (you're paying for the minute, so get in and get out) and the usual crowd (too lazy, poor, or disorganized to have internet at home) didn't exactly encourage crowd scoping. I'd always sort of zipped in, did what I had to do, and left before running up too high a bill.

And here, all this time, behind the counter, was this good-looking guy. I wondered how long he'd been watching me.

"Do you need a light?"

His voice jolted me out of my reverie. I looked up. His blue eyes were looking straight at mine, his hand holding out a lighter.

I reached forward and lit my cigarette.

"Thanks," I said, nervously. I couldn't stop staring at him.

Nervous, inconsequential conversation. I think I asked

him where he was from, I think he asked me. Something about where he lived, something about how long I'd be in town. The whole time, I kept trying to figure out how to make it real, how to say something that would somehow tell him all about me, that would cleanly communicate who I was and what I wanted—him, on my bed, wearing as little as possible.

But instead it was forgettable bar conversation. With a little bit of flirting. With a little extra eye contact, but still forgettable with charm thrown in.

My one leap of hope came when our cigarettes were finished. What next? What would he say? What would he do? We both stared at our cigarette buts, ground into the sidewalk, and then looked at each other. What next, indeed?

"I should probably get back to—" he started to say, but then he stopped, because I kissed him.

Our mouths dirty with smoke, our tongues dry with nerves, but a kiss just the same. My lips on his, my tongue in his mouth, feeling his mouth, the inside of his body, the warmth, the wet. He wrapped his arms around me and pulled me against him, and we stood there, outside the Internet café, on the corner of one street meeting another, as our bodies did the same. I felt his strength in the lean arms and the slim waist, I pulled him tight to me, as though I'd known him before, as though we'd had dates and coffees and dinners and conversations, as though I knew this body, as though this body knew mine.

We kissed. Tasting each other. Oblivious to the door swinging open and shut behind us, ignoring the people walking by, the ice cream stand next door. It was as though I'd been hungry for him, and now I was starting to feel fed.

Too soon it ended, he pulling back his face to look at mine, the blue eyes inches away, the mouth suddenly too far, leaving mine suddenly too empty. I looked at him, anxious, apprehensive—would there be a rebuttal? A dismissal?

Instead, he smiled. Eyes wrinkling around the edges.

"I've got to go back inside," he said.

I nodded obediently.

"Care to continue our conversation?"

I grinned.

"Of course."

We filed back inside, him to his desk, me to mine, and logged on.

* * *

Only this time, now that we'd met and shared a street corner, the conversation had no choice but to feel different. It wasn't that it was less intense, or that the boxes blinked less, but it was just different. It wasn't about sex and fantasy—now we were interested in ourselves.

Perversely, as the interchange became less "intimate," it grew more personal. The "getting to know you" bullshit from our first awkward cigarette became the "I really want to know you" of the Internet chat. Some questions, which could never be asked in front of faces and eyes, came quick and heavy in front of our monitors. We were in the same room, but for all intents and purposes, we could have been miles apart. Our attentions were focused solely and intensely on our monitors and the respective brain at the other end.

With his frankness and charm, it didn't take long until he'd found out about me and I about him. Only his life (student, brother, son) seemed a lot simpler to explain than mine (stripper, sister, daughter).

He seemed to take the revelations pretty well. He seemed intrigued and turned on, and maybe only a little intimidated. As usual, he asked questions about it, which didn't surprise me, but he told me he'd never been to a strip bar before, which did.

His questions entertained me while my answers apparently did the same for him, and, before I realized it, his shift was over.

"Want to get a drink?" he typed.

"Absolutely," I replied.

It had only been a couple hours since our shared cigarette break, but this time, as we exited the building, it felt completely different. We interlocked arms, with only the slightest hint of unfamiliarity, and made our way to a bar down the street, the speed and fervor of our conversation mimicking the one we'd just shared online.

Over drinks at the bar, our conversation maintained its level of intimacy, the only marked change being that now we were facing each other, not our computers, and our bodies were sharing the same space. Thanks to the lubrication of alcohol, we quickly achieved a level of physical comfort perhaps reserved for people who have actually been dating (rather than only having met each other online a few hours before)—the only change being that every time a part of his body touched mine, I became incredibly aware of just how close he and I were sitting, and of how very much I still wanted him naked in my bed.

It didn't feel like we'd been there long—the only testament to our efforts the empty glasses on the table—before he suggested leaving. From that point, it felt like a matter of minutes (which, in actuality, it probably was) until we were making our way down the street, up the stairs, and into my apartment (the logical option, since I lived closer).

We collapsed together on the couch, finally at liberty to do the things we'd wanted to do for hours—or at least, part of them. I tore at his clothes, he tore at mine. I kissed him and licked him and bit him and grabbed him. He did the same to me. There was something about his neck that drove me wild. It was so smooth, and he had the most incredible tendon running

90

into his collarbone, and I kept running my teeth over it, and then down his shoulder, wanting to eat it and swallow it and consume it.

He couldn't stop touching my breasts. Marveling at the way (apparently) they fit perfectly in his hands, he couldn't take his hands off them…squeezing, pulling, holding, stroking. He ran his fingers around the circle of my nipple, he ran his tongue across the tip, he pulled me to him so that they filled his mouth, and he pushed me away so he could look at them, resting in his hand.

We grabbed and we held and we licked and we touched until I knew what I wanted to do, and I was drunk enough to ask for it.

"Do you want a lap dance?"

He froze and looked up slowly, my breasts still in his hands. He stared at me, eyes wide.

"Are you serious?"

I grinned. "Sure. You've never had one, right?"

He shook his head.

"That's what I thought. Only we do it my way."

"Okay." He smiled. "What do I have to do?"

I became director. This was the lap dance I'd always wanted to do.

I put him in a chair in the middle of the room. Only he was naked, his arms tied behind his back with a loose scarf. I didn't want to hurt him, I just wanted him unable to touch me, or himself.

I go to the stereo and quickly paw through the CDs to find my favorite one. I put it on. You just watch me while I watch you, out of the corner of my eye, smiling to myself. This was one of those fantasies I'd never even realized how badly I'd wanted until just now, when suddenly it felt like I'd been wanting it every day of my life.

The beats came on and I stood in front of you, still

halfway clothed. All the "outerwear" was on the floor, near the couch, leaving me in underwear, and shoes—which were heels I had just put on.

You stared at me, and I stared back. Then I started to move. The music filled the room.

Mississippi in the middle of a dry spell...

I swayed in front of him, moving my hips to the left, to the right, to the left, to the right. My hands ran over my body, cupping the breasts he so desired, licking my fingers, tracing trails of saliva across the nipples, pinching them to make them hard and red, pulling them in front his face.

"Lick them," I said.

Lick them, he did.

...Black velvet with that slow Southern style, a new religion that'll bring you to your knees, Black velvet if you please...

Slowly, I lowered my hips onto his lap, but just barely, just teasing, just grazing his skin with mine, and then up again, hovering, as though the movement was effortless, as though I weighed nothing at all. My hips slinked back and forth, side to side, as his cock rose to find me.

...The way he moved, it was a sin, so sweet and true, Always wanting more, he'd leave you longing for...

All of him there, on display, arms stretched back, legs pressed together, skin white and glistening, his hard cock pointing straight at me. I wanted it inside me, oh, yes, I did, but not yet. Not yet.

...Black velvet and that little boy smile, Black velvet in that slow southern style...

Shifting back and forth, sliding up and down, finally letting his cock press against my damp underwear, letting my breasts slip into his open mouth, my pelvis tilted forward, his tilted up, his cock hard in the space between us. I start to grind against him. His arms strain against the fabric.

"No. You can't." I smiled at him, my finger tracing the line of his lips. "You've got to be a good boy."

I pick up the pace. You pick up the pace. You shove yourself at me. I suck my stomach in, push my breasts out. You grab them in your mouth like a hungry child. Your face is red. Mine is getting sweaty. My underwear is wet. Your cock is starting to glisten.

The blood is pounding in my ears. The track has changed, become a Britney Spears number. I take the opportunity to wrap my arms around your chest, to pull myself tighter against you. We are barely breathing, focused so hard on moving together, into each other, closer, faster.

I can't stand it anymore. I tear off what's left of my underwear—now a soggy mess—and drop it on the floor.

Now I'm just wearing heels. Nothing else. I'm as naked as you.

I want your cock inside me. I want it inside me now.

I want to feel it, I want you to feel me, I want to make you burst inside me.

I want to feel the pressure. I want to feel it now.

I want you inside me. All of you inside me.

I spread my legs and shove you inside. Your hips jerk as you press deeper. I wrap myself around you, grabbing the back of the chair. Shoving. Splitting. Squeezing.

I'm grabbing at your back. You are straining at your fabric, but I tied the knot too well. I can feel you tearing me in two. I want more. I want you deeper. Farther. All of you in all of me.

And then you're coming, spasming and bucking, and it's like I'm riding a bull, and I'm holding on for dear life, and I want more.

And then you shudder, and I shudder, and we collapse and contract, and I fall against you. Only now do we remember to breathe—and we do, slowly at first, gulps of air.

Feeling each other as our lungs inhale and exhale in synchronized need.

I untie you.

You wrap your arms around me and slowly stand up, holding me to you. You carry me onto the bed. We fall into it, together.

I'm still wearing my heels. You're still wearing nothing at all.

Which makes it that much easier to do it, again.

R U Out Tonight?

HIM: R U out tonight?

HER: No, I'm not. I'm at home. Who is this?

HIM: U don't recognize the number? thought u put it in yr phone.

HER: Guess I didn't…Who R U?

HIM: U don't remember me?! ;) I remember yr beautiful eyes like it was yesterday…

HER: Oh yeah? Thanks. But, um, where did we meet?

HIM: I bought you a drink. I held your hand. I almost kissed you but got shy. :(

HER: Really? When was this?

HIM: Can't believe you don't remember. Guys do this to you all the time? & I just wanted to see you again…

HER: Yr very sweet but I still don't know who you are.

HIM: Brown hair, brown eyes…couldn't stop staring at yr lips. Makes me want to see those lips again…

HER: Oh yeah?

HIM: Can't stop thinking about those lips & what they must feel like.

HER: Yr very sweet. Thanks.

HIM: So? Any chance to buy U another drink? To get U out of the house?

HER: Oh, I don't know. I'm sort of in bed already.

HIM: What R U wearing? ;)

HER: :) Ha ha. Not very much!

HIM: Perfect. So U don't have to change! ;)

HER: Funny. But I can't leave the house like this!

HIM: Who said anything about leaving the house…? ;)

HER: Oh yeah? U think U can just come over and get in

95

bed with me? Just like that?

HIM: Oh no, not just like THAT. There R many things I'd do 2 U first, don't worry! & many things U could do 2 me...

HIM: Does that scare U?

HER: Not really. I just think it's funny that you've never texted me b4.

HIM: I think U make me shy.

HER: Why's that? Because I make u want to do things you've never done b4?

HIM: ...Yeah. I guess so. R U still in bed?

HER: Yes.

HIM: Think I can come get in bed with U?

HER: I have to think about it...

HIM: Will U kiss me in yr bed?

HER: Don't know. U might have to buy me another drink first!

HIM: I can do that. I can do lots of things if it gets me in bed with u. ;)

HER: Really? Like what?

HIM: Dunno. What U want. Dancing? Dinner? I'll even wear a suit. ;)

HER: Ha ha. Funny. U don't have to wear a suit!

HIM: Oh, honey, I'd rather wear nothing at all.

HER: Ah. I see. :) So U R naked and I am almost naked and then what happens?

HIM: I'd run my tongue down your thighs...

HER: & then?

HIM: & then I'd run my tongue between yr legs...

HER: & then?

HIM: & then I'd slip my fingers between yr legs & squeeze yr breasts with my other hand.

HER: Where is yr tongue now? Is it still between my legs?

HIM: Oh, baby, my tongue is EVERYWHERE. ;) U can't even tell where it's going or where it's been anymore! I'm btw yr legs & btw yr breasts & across yr stomach & down yr neck…& just up & down yr whole body…

HER: Yum. :)

HIM: That's exactly what I'm thinking! ;) I bet u taste amazing…

HER: Wouldn't know, never tried! ;)

HIM: Oh yeah? I'll have 2 make u.

HER: Yeah? What else do u want 2 make me do?

HIM: I want 2 make you cum. I want 2 feel u come while I am inside u.

HER: What part of u is inside which part of me…? ;)

HIM: My hard cock is inside u, in yr super wet pussy…and yr kisses are all over my face.

HER: And where r my hands?

HIM: Hmm. Good question! ;) 4 fingers are in my ass & one hand is cupping my balls… :) do you like that?

HER: Sounds pretty good. :) What do I feel like when yr inside?

HIM: Oh, u feel amazing. I could just die. U are totally wet and smooth and like hot silk…

HER: & how do you feel?

HIM: I have never been so hard. aching. on top of U, swinging back and forth, yr feet on my shoulders…

HER: Sounds hot! :)

HIM: Baby, u have no idea. :)

HER: And what do I do?

HIM: Oh shit, I forgot about you! :)

HER: U forgot?! How can U forget about me? ;)

HIM: Cuz I'm too busy thinking about how to make you feel good!

HER: But what about ME making YOU feel good?

HIM: You will. Making you feel good will make me feel

good. U don't have to do a thing, baby.

HER: But what if I want to? What if I get off on getting you off?

HIM: Then we'll work something out! :)

HER: Ah, I see. Gotcha. :) So where does all this happen?

HIM: Hm…I was hoping you'd let me in your bed if I promised to make you feel good enough…

HER: I'll think about it! :)

HIM: So where do u want to do it?

HER: So maybe we just do it on the floor?

HIM: Where?

HER: In the kitchen? :)

HIM: Ah, now yr cooking with gas! :)

HER: Ha ha. Dork. Ok. So we're in the kitchen…ha ha—and I'm wearing an apron with nothing else!

HIM: Oh, perfect! :) Sounds hot.

HER: I'm wearing my pink apron & nothing else. U R wearing nothing, of course. Want to save time.

HIM: Honey, if I'm with you, I'm not in any rush…

HER: Aw, yr sweet…

HIM: But yeah, in this case, I'm nekkid. ;)

HER: Cool. Ok. So U R on the floor and I'm on top of U?

HIM: Yeah. Sure. Then what?

HER: I start rubbing your cock against my clitoris until I'm so wet, I'm dripping all over you…

HIM: & on my hands! On my hands & down my arms & you drip down yr smooth white thighs & in my mouth & baby, U R super sweet & it runs over my face…

HER: & then I lean down & I lick myself off yr face…do U like that?

HIM: Oh god, baby, that is hot. U bet I like it.

HER: :)

HIM: & then I fuck u again in yr kitchen in that sexy pink apron! ;)

HER: Right. Of course! & then you put the apron on & then I fuck u! ;)

HIM: Wow, that's a lot of fucking!

HER: Isnt that what u want?

HIM: Of course! :) Who doesn't? With a hot chick like u?

HER: Right. With a hot chick like me! :)

HIM: Now it's yr turn.

HER: My turn? What do u mean?

HIM: What do u want to do 2 me…? :)

HER: Ah, I see! Hmmm…I don't know.

HIM: Don't believe it. Come on. Tell me something.

HER: Ok…but u promise not to laugh?

HIM: No. ;)

HER: :) It's like super girly & stuff.

HIM: So I'll laugh. Tell me.

HER: Ok. I wanna take a bath with you.

HIM: A bath?

HER: Yeah, a bath. I've got this big tub & I always use it alone & it seems like such a waste, u know…?

HIM: You mean like a big bubble bath, like in the movies?

HER: Yeah, exactly. We'll fill it up all the way…make the water really hot…keep the lights off…

HIM: I like the sound of that. Go on.

HER: Well, we get in 2gether. Obviously. & we sink down under the water. & the tub is big but not that big, u know? So we're all kind of on top of each other. Well, not really on top b/c I am at one end & u r at the other…

HIM: Go on.

HER: So my legs R wrapped around your waist and your legs R on either side of my hips…

HIM: Sounds hot! :)

HER: Totally! :) But the water is up around our shoulders

& it's all full of foam from the bubble bath so we cant see anything under the water.

HIM: But u know I'm sooo hard… ;)

HER: Yes, & u know I'm wet, but of course everything is!

HIM: LOL.

HER: So first we're sitting like that & we're facing each other & there is just the sound of water & we're breathing sort of heavy cuz it's hot…

HIM: Yeah…? How hot?

HER: It's totally steamy…from the water & from us, of course.

HIM: Yum. Then what?

HER: After a while we get bored, at least I do, so I sort of pull myself up & crawl over onto u…

HIM: So yr drowning me?

HER: Ha ha. No, silly, I'm kissing you…

HIM: Aw. OK.

HER: & I can feel you btw my legs…

HIM: Oh yeah? ;) Naughty girl!

HER: U know it! & then I reach down & slip u inside me…

HIM: & everything is wet, inside & out…

HER: :) Exactly. & u have yr arms around me & yr holding me close & I have got my hands around yr neck & your shoulders & everything is slippery…

HIM: & it feels so good…

HER: Totally. :)

HIM: & I keep u afloat…til you get cold…& then we flip sides…& u are sitting back down & I am over u…and I put my fingers between yr legs…

HER: Sounds lovely!

HIM: & I'm licking the water off yr breasts…

HER: & I'm biting yr nipples til they get all red & hard…

HIM: oh yeah? Thought I was doing that 2 U!

HER: We can take turns! ;)

HIM: Ok, fine. We take turns. :) & then I grab u out of the damn tub b/c I want 2 fuck u in a towel…

HER: :) We can do that on my bed. I don't mind a little water on my sheets… ;)

HIM: Perfect. So I carry u out of the bathroom, wrapped in yr towel like a pig in a blanket… ;)

HER: Ha ha. Yr funny.

HIM: :) So now I've got u on the bed…

HER: Yeah, & I'm all tangled in the towels & we're all wet & we're naked…

HIM: & we're fucking 4 like the 10th time that night!

HER: Just the way u like it…

HER: U got it, little girl! ;)

HER: God, talking to u makes this bed seem so lonely…

HIM: I'm not god, u know… ;) How big is yr bed?

HER: Big enuff for 2 people! ;) But also big enuff 4 a girl that likes 2 spread out… ;)

HIM: Oh yeah? Are u spread out?

HER: ;)

HIM: Are yr legs spread?

HER: ;)

HIM: where are yr hands?

HER: Well, 1 is texting u…

HIM: And where is the other 1?

HER: :)

HIM: Oh, perfect…are u getting off?

HER: It feels good but I don't usually come without my vibrator…

HIM: So where is your vibrator?

HER: Under the bed…I keep it in a box…

HIM: Well, get it out of the box then! :)

HER: Ok, ok. Dictator! ;)

101

HIM: :)

HER: Ok, it's out of the box.

HIM: & it's btw yr legs?

HER: :)

HIM: Batteries charged? Full power?

HER: :)

HIM: Yum. How does it feel?

HER: It feels really good…like always.

HIM: Do you keep it on yr clit or do you push it inside?

HER: Hmm…usually I keep it on my clit. Sometimes I push it inside.

HIM: What's yr favorite?

HER: My favorite? :) My favorite is when I have it on my clit & a cock inside of me…

HIM: My cock, right? ;)

HER: Of course!

HIM: So here's what I want u 2 do…

HER: Yeah?

HIM: Stop texting me for a minute.

HER: :(

HIM: No, listen, just 4 a minute. Now take your other hand & slip a finger inside. Make it go deep inside. Shove it in, curve it, so that it curves up against u. Move it in & out, pressing against that soft part…

HER: K.

HIM: Put the phone down and use the other hand 4 the vibrator. I want u to pretend that finger is my cock…Ok? I'll wait… ;)

HER: K.

HIM: Waiting… :)

HIM: … :)

HIM: I'm imagining what u look like. What it feels like. Does it feel good... ;) Do I feel good? ;)

HIM: …

HIM: … God, I'm getting so hard just imagining what yr doing over there. Poor lonely girl in bed by herself… :) Good thing you've got me between yr legs… ;)

HER. I'm back. ;)

HIM: Hi there. :) Welcome back! How was it?

HER: mmmmmmmm… :)

HIM: That good, huh?

HER: Better! :)

HIM: Did I feel good? :)

HER: Honey, u felt great… I'm still feeling kinda dizzy from it all.

HIM: Did u come? Did u? Did u?

HER: Oh YEAH! You bet I did! :)

HIM: What did it feel like? Tell me, tell me!

HER: Oh, baby, it felt great. Super fucking great.

HIM: How many fingers did you push inside?

HER: Only 1. 1 is enough if you know what to do with it… ;)

HIM: & I bet u do, u naughty girl!

HER: :) I did it just like u told me 2!

HIM: What turned u on the most? The vibrator outside or the finger inside?

HER: Seriously?

HIM: Yes, duh! Tell me!

HER: Uh…

HIM: Tell me!

HER: Knowing u were on the other end waiting 4 me…

HIM: For real?!

HER: Yeah. :)

HIM: Aw. Now U R being sweet! :)

HER: :) If I'm so sweet, dontcha think u owe me?

HIM: Depends on what I owe u… ;)

HER: Well, now I think it's yr turn…

HIM: My turn 4 what?

HER: U know. Yr turn.

HIM: …OH. I get it. :) OK. My turn!

& I get 2 tell u how 2 do it!

HIM: :) Sounds delicious, baby girl. What do u want me 2 do?

HER: Where R U? R U in bed, 2?

HIM: If u want me 2 be…

HER: No, come on. Where R U? 4 real?

HIM: Isn't it more romantic if I'm at home…in my bed that's 2 big 4 me?

HER: :) Well, of COURSE, but not if yr lying. Where R U really?

HIM: OK. Don't be angry. I'm @ a boring indie rock show.

HER: LOL. REALLY?

HIM: Yeah. So don't disappear! Yr keeping it from being totally boring. :)

HER: Ha ha. Funny. What band is it?

HIM: Dunno. promised my roommate I'd see the band that's playing after the guys that R on now. Wanna kill these guys. They're awful.

HER: :) Perfect. So u don't mind missing the show…?

HIM: Oh, please, tell me how I can! :)

HER: K. Go 2 the bathroom, pls.

HIM: 1 sec…

HIM: Alright. I'm in the bathroom. In a stall. Door closed.

HER: R yr pants around yr ankles?

HIM: :)

HER: Is yr cock sticking out of yr underwear?

HIM: I'm not wearing underwear… ;)

HER: GROSS! Ha ha. Just kidding. Hot. R U hard yet?

HIM: Honey, I've been hard 4ever! 4 U! ;)

HER: :) Super. Oh, btw, does it smell bad in the

bathroom?

HIM: Nah. Why?

HER: Just want 2 picture it perfectly! Is the stall standard size? R U against the wall?

HIM: Standard. Yes.

HER: :) Alright. Can u get the phone to stay on yr left shoulder? Like w/ yr head? Or is it 2 small?

HIM: Nothing about me is 2 small! ;) Esp not now! & yes, my phone is big & old skool, so no problem. But I cant text u with my shoulder…

HER: That's ok. Just want 2 hear u breathe.

HIM: Wait, u want me 2 call u?

HER: Yeah. But not yet. I don't want 2 talk on the phone, just want 2 hear u breathe.

HIM: Uh, ok…

HER: So this is what I want & then I want u to call…I want 1 hand on yr cock, u know what 2 do, I hope! ;) Then put yr other hand on yr balls. I want u to feel yr balls getting more & more swollen…

HIM: OK. I can do that. But only 4 u! ;)

HER: Wait, 1 more thing, I want you to lick yr right hand.

HIM: OK.

HER: But wait, this is important. Close yr eyes & lick yr hand…imagine it's me & my tongue, k?

HIM: :) I could do that over & over.

HER: U can do it 3 times. ;)

HIM: OK. Done. Now what?

HER: Now u call me…and u do it!

HIM: OK.

HIM: Did u hear everything?

HER: :)

HIM: Did it turn you on?

HER: U have no idea… ;)

HIM: REALLY? Just the sound of my breathing?

HER: …& knowing what u were doing…did u think of me when u were doing it?

HIM: :)

HER: where is the cum now? Is it on yr hand?

HIM: It's sort of on the wall… ;)

HER: Ha ha. That's perfect. :) Can I ask u something kinky?

HIM: Sure.

HER: Leave it there.

HIM: Of course. U thought I'd clean it up? ;)

HER: And now tell me where you are, exactly.

HIM: U mean, which club?

HER: Which stall. ;)

HIM: ………..why? u want to come lick my cum off the wall?

HER: Nah. I want 2 make u come again on the wall. Only I wanna be there when it happens.

HIM: Really?!

HER: Yes. I make house calls. Only in this case, restroom calls. :) & just 4 u…so tell me where u are & I'll find u.

HIM: Sounds fucking hot. I can't wait.

HER: Neither can i. :)

Sorry

I can't believe you broke up with me.

I can't believe it's over, and it's over because you decided that's how it would be. You decided you had enough, and that was it, finito. The end. Exit.

We'd barely even got started, and you already had enough.

Well, let me tell you something, you're going to regret it. You know why? Because you're never going to find another girl like me. You're never going to find another girl who feels the way I do, who kisses the way I do, who goes down on you the way I did.

How quickly you've forgotten. Don't you remember I was the best head you ever had? How is it that you've forgotten and I remember every fucking second?

I remember that time when I came by your apartment early in the morning, right after my flight got in, and you were still sleeping, and I went over and sat on the bed, and you sat up to hold me, and as I leaned forward into your arms, I looked down, and saw how hard you were, poking up like that through the blanket, and I looked at you and laughed, and you laughed back, saying that with me, it never took much time. And then you asked me if I'd touch it, and I did, because I always did, and I wrapped my hand around you but I never stopped looking in your eyes, and the second my hand wrapped around your cock, you blinked, and then your eyes opened sort of halfway, and you had this drunk look, this drugged look you always got when I touched you there, and I started to rub you, and you started to moan, and I rubbed faster, feeling the skin slide back and forth, until I could tell

107

you were just starting to leak your precum, and then I broke eye contact to lean forward and slip you in my mouth, and then I finished you while you grabbed the blanket in your fists and you moaned and you sighed and you begged me not to stop, not to stop, cause you were coming, coming, coming, and then you did, the sweet bitterness feeling my mouth, and then I sat up, and you wrapped your arms around me, and then you pulled me down on the bed, and we lay like that as the sun came through the window and covered us in light, and I don't think I've ever felt so warm in my life.

Or the first time we had sex? You didn't want to. You wanted to wait, but I couldn't wait anymore. I wanted you like I'd never wanted anyone before. You didn't have to fuck me, I just wanted to feel you, and somehow you had this self control and you said you could wait, and I don't know how you did it, because I knew how turned on you were because you were hard all the time we were together, but somehow you said you could wait, but I couldn't, and then we were lying in bed together, and we were each on our sides, facing each other, and I was holding your cock in my hand, and I was rubbing back and forth, giving you one of my fabulous handjobs, and then I scootched myself just a little bit closer and tilted my hips just the right way, until somehow, by accident, totally by accident, the little tip of your cock, when I pulled my hand to the top, was just touching the lips of my pussy, just oh so barely hovering around the edges, and as my hand accelerated, my hips somehow tilted just a bit more, and then I was just a bit closer, and you were just a little more inside, and then a little more inside, and then there was no getting around it, you were inside me, in the tunnel of my insides, pink wet flesh against pink wet flesh, and you moaned in my ear, "oh my god," you said, and I pushed myself closer towards you, until you were all the way in, and there was no way you had any self-control left, and then I kept shoving my hips until you started shoving yours, and then we were having proper goddamn sex, and it was the best, most intense thing I could ever remember having felt, and it was just pure magic...

But somehow you forgot that. You've forgotten the amazing chemistry we have, the way it felt when I sat on your lap the first time, and you wrapped your hands around me, and the train came, but neither of us wanted to get up, and even though we didn't say anything out loud, we were both totally relieved when we saw it was just an out of service line and not our train at all, so we could keep sitting like that for another few minutes, feeling each other's heat and body...

Either you've forgotten what that was like, or you've decided that's not important for you anymore. You don't care about having sex that leaves your entire body tingling. You don't care about coming in my mouth in a way that leaves your body completely collapsed as you float on waves of bliss—those were your words, in case you've also forgotten that.

How could it not matter to you? Whatever happened between us, how could you have so little respect for this kind of chemistry, for this kind of energy, that you can just walk away from it? You think you're going to find another girl who will make you feel like this? You think you'll find another girl who will feel like this about you? You're crazy. You won't. These things come along once in a lifetime.

Or, maybe, you've decided you don't need sex anymore. You're just going to be friends with women. Maybe you'll be a priest. Maybe you'll go gay. Because it's not possible that you'd walk away from me for anything less.

I'm not a slut but I've had enough sex to know when it's good, and with you it was really, really good. Even that first time, when it wasn't really fucking but just sort of feeling...I can still remember what that was like. And the first time we fucked? When you got on top of me, and then you got behind me, and you were so big and hard but it just felt perfect, and you were behind me, and you had your fingers around so that you could finger me, and you fucked me and you fingered me, and I didn't move, I couldn't move, I just had my head in the pillow, and I used every bit of traction I could find to shove back against you, to keep my hips locked in position, while my thighs quivered and my clitoris swelled, and your cock rammed into me so hard, I could feel your balls swinging back and forth and then I came so hard I leaked all over your bed and you had to change the sheet?

You told me you'd never made someone do that before.

I told you no one had me do that before.

That was the truth.

No one felt as good to hold. No one made me want to hold them as much. No one made me want to jump them and rip their clothes off and drag them into bed as much. I couldn't stop thinking about the way your cock felt and the way it looked when it pressed against your pants, and that time we were cooking in the kitchen, and I sat on the counter, and you leaned against me, and I wrapped my legs around your waist, and I kissed you so deeply, I felt like I might fall into your mouth, and there, with the smell of the potatoes in the oven, your cock got so hard, you unzipped your pants, and fucked me, just like that, as I sat on the counter, my legs wrapped around you, and we were both so nervous your roommates would come, but we couldn't stop, not even for the few seconds it would have taken to get to your bedroom. We couldn't stop, and you fucked me as my head hit against the cupboards, but I didn't feel anything, not a thing but your cock between my legs and your lips against mine, and the way your breath felt on my face as you panted.

Oh god, we had the best sex. In every room in your house—but don't tell your roommates.

And now it's over, and you'll never have that kind of sex again, so I guess your roommates are safe now.

It's funny, now your roommates are nicer to me than you are. At least, they pretend they want to talk to me when I call. Or that time we were supposed to meet but you didn't show up, and you just left a message that you were sick, but when I called your house, you weren't there, and your roommate was like, oh no, he's ok, I think he's at Sally's.

And I was like, oh, at Sally's? Does she fuck you as well as I do? Does she feel as good on the inside? Is her skin as soft? You loved my skin. You couldn't stop touching it. And when you go for walks in the park together, does she pull you behind a tree and let you put your hands under her shirt while you tell her how perfect her breasts are and then, when she feels you getting hard, does she unzip your pants and go down on you behind one of those big oak trees? Giving you head like a porn star, you said, making you feel so good that you forgot to be nervous about anyone watching...and then the best part, of course, would be when I'd stand up again, and you'd look at me confused, because you hadn't come yet, but you were aching to and you wanted me to finish but you didn't want to ask because at least you'd pretend you were nice guy, and I would smile at you, and then I'd step closer, and lift my skirt up just a little, slide my underwear to the side, and let you push your way in, and you'd pant into my ear, and you'd say, my god, how amazing it all felt, and we'd fuck like that, in the woods, in total silence, just listening to the sound of our breath and the leaves falling, and I'd grab the tree bark in my hands to pull myself to you as tightly as possible, and there is always something so perfect about coming in the middle of the woods.

Did you do that with Sally? Do you do that with Sally?

I remember that time we went to the Salvation Army because you were looking for pants, and I was standing at the racks, flipping through the clothes, trying to find something your size, and you just stood behind me, with your arms around me, looking like the sweetest, most-in-love boyfriend ever, and the whole time, I could feel your dick hard between your legs, pressing against my ass, and we walked through the store like children, like Siamese twins, with your arms tight around me, you were like my appendage, and I remember wondering if you were doing that because you didn't want the other people in the store to see your hard-on or if you were doing it because you just wanted to feel me so badly. But I didn't care, I just sort of loved it, and then we went into the dressing room, which was in the middle of the store, so that you could try on the pants, but when you took off your pants, you were so hard, I couldn't resist, and I let you fuck me right there, in the middle of that friggin Salvation Army, and it was fantastic sex, like it always was with you.

I wonder if you'll ever get it that good again. Sometimes I wonder if I'll ever get it that good again...

But you know what? It will never be like that, but it doesn't matter, since you're not who I thought you were. And if you're really what you seem to be, then, sorry, I can do better.

And you know what? I already have. Remember that guy I met a year ago? The one you joked about, I think maybe you said he was hulking? Ha. Well, I always did love big guys...I think you were one of my few exceptions! Turns out that for such a "hulk," he's pretty damn good with his body, and, unlike you, sex isn't just about getting off. He loves to fuck, of course, but he loves everything else about it, too. He even likes to play games together, and he doesn't think it's weird or kinky or fucked up...and we go out together, and I pull him into a corner and slip my hand inside his pants, and he puts his hand up my skirt, and he doesn't tell me I have to wait until we get home because I'm totally turning him on, so we fall into one of those booths, and we start making out, and he doesn't care if anyone is watching because he's too busy touching and kissing me, and he just feels amazing. Then he puts his fingers inside me, right there in the booth, and it's all I can do to keep from making any sound, and my head sort of falls back against the wall, and I grab his hard cock with my hand, my other hand fingers clenching the leather of the booth, and, well, we don't even have to be having sex for it to feel better than anything you've ever done to me.

So I wish you luck with Sally, or whatever her name is, and I hope you find everything you've always wanted with her, and that she's perfect in all the ways you kept reminding me that I was not. Certainly seems like life gives us what we deserve, doesn't it?

The Arrangement

We had an arrangement.

Rule 1: When I promised to dress up, he promised to fuck me.

Rule 2: When he invited, in just the right ways, I would come over, to do just the right things. He would do the same for me.

Rule 3: Any fantasies were a go. No laughing or uptight conservative reactions permitted.

Rule 4: No relationship expectations or demands.

Rule 5: Everything stayed private. No public appearances or revelations.

Rule 6: All whims were to be indulged.

That's how it worked.

Something about having a relationship takes the fun out of it. Something about watching each other brush his teeth, making coffee, doing laundry, kind of kills the mood. Something about sharing everything means feeling like you've gained nothing. Something about the guarantee to be there for each other guarantees being bored with each other.

So, hence—our arrangement. I'd never *really* had fun with someone before. Not like this. This was about fun. This was about everything we'd never done with anyone else before.

And we both kept denying that it meant anything. It was about play and experimentation. It was about keeping each other satisfied.

Which was fine in my book, because I'd probably never have had the nerve to do the things I did with him with anyone else—if it actually mattered, I'd probably freeze up like an Eskimo.

(The crazy thing, though, and I'd never tell him this, was that I didn't want to do them with anyone else. No one drove me crazy the way he did. No one made me want to get dirty and violent. No one else made me feel further away from the nice games everyone else got. I didn't want anyone else to push me up against the wall. I didn't want anyone else's sweat dripping on my skin. Everyone else got the conversation, the handholding, the pleasantries. He got me, raw. Hungry. Because he made me that way.)

It's funny how it started. We didn't start out being so unconventional. We tried to date. We tried to do it the normal way, which made sense, since we're both normal people—at least the rest of the time, with everybody else. But it didn't work.

(I'm still not sure why. Part of me thought, well, maybe according to the basic rules, we didn't "work," since we're too different or whatever. Another part of me, the part I'd never admit to him, thought that it scared the fuck out of us how well we worked, and since nothing really functions when you're scared, we didn't stand a chance.

We made each other too damn nervous and afraid because it was like standing on the edge of this great big chasm and looking straight down and not wanting to breath or shift or adjust a rib because then you could fall—and what was scarier than a straight fall without a safety net? It was hard to relax when we were around each other, to be ourselves, because, oh my god, what if being ourselves fucked this perfect thing up…and there is no better way to fuck it up than feeling like that.)

So we fucked it up. Then, like mature adults, we politely pressed ESC on our relationship with a smattering of tears, and that was the end of that.

Only it's hard to disentangle from such an attraction, since all I wanted was to wrap my hands around him and see him naked, on his back, on his bed, as I stood over him, watching his body, seeing his body, feeling his hands around my calves, wetness dripping down my thighs…

But I didn't get that.

All I got, as a condolence, was his friendship. He didn't want to "lose me," he said.

At first, we played it like a game where you know the rules and pretend you don't know the outcome. But, my god, why was it that I still thought of him whenever my hand went between my legs, and why was it that thinking of him always sent my hand between my legs?

The worst part was that he encouraged it. He seemed to want it, as well—but he didn't know what to do with his feelings and his desire to see me naked on his bed, his cock between my legs, making my pussy drip, so he would slip away and hide, disappearing for weeks, but then, goddammit, we'd be in the same place at the same time again.

Everything was "over," but I couldn't shake the feeling that we hadn't even started yet. I wanted him, in the flesh. I wanted to hear his moans, I wanted to rub myself against him, I wanted to feel him hard against my thigh, between my legs, I wanted his hands all over my breasts, I wanted his lips between my teeth. I wanted to make him pant. I wanted to make him lose his breath.

Then there I was, out of nowhere, invited to his house, and I had a hard time making platonic conversation because the roaring in my ears made me feel like I was in the middle of a hurricane. Even though I tried to play by the rules, because I knew what I *should* do—he pulled me down on the couch as I was trying to leave, and, despite my attempts to rationalize and deny it—we had fantastic sex.

Oh god, nothing I did could make me forget him, and

these little tastes just sent me home with a clearer vision of what I wanted. The more I glimpsed what could be, the more I wanted to yank that curtain aside and see it all. I wanted to gorge, to devour, to consume. I wanted him to split me in two while my fingers tore holes across his skin.

Our next encounter was at a concert, at a chastely public venue, and we made the type of conversation that was totally boring and innocuous, yet my face couldn't stop flushing, and I didn't know what to do with my hands, and I felt all nervous, and didn't know what to say, and I laughed at all the wrong times, and it felt so wrong because it felt so right.

I wanted the room to empty. I wanted everyone to go home so he could fuck me on the stage. I wanted a spotlight on his body, on the skin about which I couldn't stop fantasizing, on the cock I wanted in my mouth, in my hand, and between my legs. I wanted to see him, between the amplifiers, naked, on his back, moaning as my tongue ran over his skin. I wanted to feel his cock spasming in my mouth, his balls hard in my hand, while his fingers shoved themselves inside me and the disco ball kept spinning its patterns across the ceiling.

But the room didn't empty, and I didn't say goodbye when I left, and I didn't see him again for two weeks.

C'est de rigeur, n'est-ce pas?

So I put him out of my head. I knew it was a crazy junkie addiction, something I knew better than to indulge. It was a hunger I'd never be able to satisfy, a stupid fixation on a stupid boy, all the more stupid because I had other boys to play nice with. But I kept comparing them to him, and he kept coming back.

Then, he invited me over. Since I felt like I had nothing to lose, I decided to be frank. I told him I'd had this idea, for an arrangement. I told him what I wanted. I told him what the rules would be. I told him what I would expect, and what I wouldn't, and that's how it started.

Floodgates—open. Imagination—on fire. Desire—in place.

A relationship, with just the perks. None of the sloth.

He agreed. He wanted to play.

Rules 1-6 were established.

And it worked. It gave me the sexual affair I'd always wanted but never got to have—outside of my own head. I finally had the courage to ask for what I wanted, and he got to have me without any of the complications or expectations that scared him away.

The first night of the arrangement, I could barely wait. I pulled out the garters. The thigh highs. The super skimpy black lace underwear. The dress I bought thinking of him, even though that was one of those weeks where we weren't talking. The heels. And then I realized we weren't having a dinner date. This wasn't right, at all. No need to play it safe. Every need to take it all the way. So I took it all off (except for the heels) and put on a coat.

It was time to stop compromising, to hold nothing back. I had no reason to be afraid. I could do everything I'd always imagined doing, and he'd be right there, all the way. This had the potential for a lot more than great sex, and I was going to take the opportunity as far as I could.

I went over to his place. I rang the bell. He opened the door. I stepped inside. I dropped the coat. He grabbed me.

It was like every bit of frustration from every one of those weeks (where we weren't talking) and those moments (where we were) crashed into an accelerated moment of fire.

I kept my shoes on but we took his clothes off as quickly as we could. I wanted his body underneath mine. I wanted to taste his flesh. I wanted to feel him between my teeth, against my fingernails, and oh god, of course, I wanted him inside me. His tongue on the inside of my thighs was just a joke. A teaser. A torment. His lips on my neck, breasts, ear just made me squirm, made me twist and turn and pull him to me. I wanted to fall on the floor with him. I wanted him to fall onto me. I wanted him to fall into me. I wanted him to take me from behind and from on top and from the side, and I wanted to grab him and devour him, and I wanted to lose myself in the hunger that was all consuming.

I was shaking from desire.

I wanted him to feed me.

I wanted him to fill me up. Satiate. Satisfy. No seduction necessary. No foreplay needed. The past six months had been foreplay. The past six months had been our dance of "do we" or "do we not." And now it was "we do."

Time had gone too slowly, and now it still wasn't going fast enough. I still couldn't get enough—of him.

We managed to make it to the bedroom, somehow. In the midst of all the grabbing, we got down the hall, and then it was strict collapse.

I was on the bottom. He was on the top. My legs spread wide. His pressed together. His lovely waist between my arms as I wrapped myself around him and pulled him down, down, down, and in, in, in. I could feel his ass clenching as his cock shoved into me, and I clenched it, in return. Come on, come on, come *on*.

It wasn't about anything any more but our bodies and the fact that we couldn't get close enough. We were parts that made a whole, and the more our sweat intermingled, the hotter it got. I couldn't get him close enough, my nails on his back, on his arms, on his ass—oh, his perfect ass. And he grabbed my breasts between his teeth, and his hands around my neck, and we were digging into each other, with a need pure and uninhibited in its desire.

Moving together, faster, faster, faster, faster, until he collapsed into me, literally, figuratively, a mess of bodies, and

I held him and panted, our breaths shuddering through our bodies, while we slowly brought ourselves down to earth.

"Will it be so good next time?" he asked.

"It will only get better," I said, grabbing his hand and pulling him up. "Come on. Shower time."

"What?" He shook his head groggily. "I don't need a shower."

"Oh yeah, you do." I grinned. "Let's go."

I dragged him off the bed and behind me into the bathroom. I turned the water on, letting the hot water start to steam behind the curtain. He walked over to the toilet and lifted the lid.

"Not yet," I said, smirking, tapping the lid back down.

"Huh?"

"But first…"

"Yeah?"

"Remember the rule? Everything we do stays just between you and me. The arrangement?"

"Yes, of course," he replied, uncertainly. "What do you have in mind?"

I smiled at him as I stepped into the path of the shower, offering him my hand. "Won't you join me in here? It's warm…"

Looking a bit bemused, he joined me in the bathtub, pulling the curtain closed behind him. I turned to look at him. God, he was beautiful. His long lean limbs starting to drip with water, his smooth skin glistening in the steam, his hair collecting pockets of water that ran down his face in rivulets, around his eyes and his now wet eyelashes. I traced my fingers across his lips, and he opened his mouth in response, and I felt the damp warmth of his mouth as my index finger slipped inside, echoing the damp warmth of our current domain.

I ran a circle around the outside of his mouth before sending my finger down his neck, down his chest, down his stomach, to his cock, which was already starting to get hard again.

"I want you to piss now," I said.

"What? In the bathtub?"

"Yes. Do it. For me. Please."

"Uh, okay. Just here?" He pointed at the drain.

"No. Here." I kneeled down and pointed at my face.

"On *you*?"

"Yes. Please." I put one hand on each of his legs and waited, feeling the strength of his calves while waiting for the heat of his insides.

It didn't take long. He started slow, awkwardly, but the drips rapidly became a stream shooting over my face, into my open mouth, across my closed eyes, mingling with the water from the shower, but still focused enough that I could taste the warm saltiness that came direct from him. I didn't move, staying frozen in place, until he'd finished, until the stream became drips again, and I leaned my head back, letting the shower rinse it all clean again. I wiped my face with my hand and opened my eyes. He was staring at me with an intensity I'd never seen before. I stared back at him. The only sound was the water hitting the porcelain and tile.

I broke the moment by sitting up straighter, running my hands up his legs, wrapping my mouth around his cock. Then the only sound was the water and his moans as I moved my tongue and my lips back and forth, firm and tight around his skin, shower droplets beating on my back, pressure building until he gave one final moan, and then my mouth was full of an entirely different fluid.

He grabbed my hand, pulling me up. We looked at each other—our hair damp around our faces, our bodies shivering slightly, either from the water not being quite hot enough or from the intensity of our desire. He was still beautiful. His fingers traced the lines of my face. I moved forward to kiss

122

him.

"No. I want to look at you."

I stepped back. I felt him looking at me. I felt the water rinsing every pore, somehow the wetness making our nakedness feel even more naked, as if the dirt that had been rinsed down the drain had been a protective layer, and now we were stripped bare. Exposed. Revealed. I couldn't look back at him. My eyes drifted down his face, to his neck and his shoulders, back up, to his ears and his hair, and his forehead. He just stared at me.

"How long have you been wanting to do that?" he asked, with the hint of a smile.

I smiled back. "I'm not sure. A long time. I just never thought it would actually happen."

He laughed. "Guess you can cross it off his list then…?" We looked at each other for a beat before he continued. "We can do it again, if you like. Another time."

I nodded.

He cleared his throat awkwardly. I waited to see what he'd say next.

"Have you got more things on that list of yours?" he asked, with a mixture of hesitation and curiosity.

I grinned. "Yes. I've got a lot more things on that list of mine."

"Great. So next time…?"

* * *

A couple nights later, the ringing of my phone woke me just as I was falling asleep.

"What are you doing?" he asked.

"I'm actually ensconced in bed. Why?"

"You should come get ensconced with me."

"Oh god, I don't know…I'm half-asleep."

123

"Ah, but you see, this is a special offer."

"Yeah? Why's that?"

"Because I'm not at home."

"You've lost me." I was starting to get irritable. Booty calls were one thing, but wake-up booty calls were another.

"Right now, I'm lying in a king size bed in a king size suite at the Hilton Park."

"What? Why? What are you doing *there*?" The Hilton Park was one of the nicest hotels in town.

"I've got the room booked all week for one of the artists on my label, but he's stuck in Boston one more night doing interviews. He's not returning until tomorrow. So it's empty. It's empty tonight…except for me…and you?"

I grinned. "You're serious?"

"Haven't you always wanted to do it in a hotel before?"

Laughing. "Darling, I've done it in hotels before."

"Yes, but not like this."

"What do him mean?"

"Well, I've, uh, never done it with, uh, an escort before…"

I was starting to figure it out. "You want me to pretend?"

I could feel the relief through the phone. "Yes. Yes. That would be amazing. Can we do that?"

"You got it."

It took about two seconds for me to get out of bed and another sixty to get dressed. Not that it was really relevant, although maybe that was part of the reason for his fantasy, I'd worked as an escort before, when I was in grad school. So I knew what to wear. I didn't have the same clothes now that I had then, but I had the same high-heeled boots, and I approximated the rest—tailored slacks, low-cut shirt, long fake fur coat, hair swept back, makeup. Although important, the clothes weren't what made the experience. I knew it was about the heels and the attitude. Everything else came off quickly, anyway.

Twenty minutes later, I knocked on the door of his suite. As though he'd been waiting on the other side, it instantly swung open and he gave me a warm smile. I gave him a cool one in return.

"Hello, I'm Sydney," I said, sweeping into the room. "Nice to meet you." I spun around—officially, seductively, powerfully—and stared him in the eyes. He looked back at me.

"I'm Tom."

(I kept the grin to myself. Even he was using a fake name.)

"I'm sorry, but I have to get the money up front." I stepped closer to him and ran a finger down his cheek, resting briefly on his mouth. "Gets it out of the way and then we can focus on everything else…"

He blinked at me. "The money?"

Again, I resisted the urge to smile. "Yes. Of course. This isn't a comp, is it?"

A knowing look slid across his face. "No, no, of course not. I'm sorry. How much did him say it was?"

"The official price is $400. I'll give you a first-time deal of $200."

"$200?!"

This time I let myself grin, but I kept it cool and collected. If he wanted to play, I'd show him how it was done.

"Yes. $200. If you don't have it now, I'll come back later."

I started to walk back towards the door.

He reached out and grabbed my arm. "No, no, that's okay. I've got it. One second."

And he really did. He pulled it out of his wallet, and I put it neatly into mine.

"Alright then." I smiled broadly. "Want to offer me a

drink?"

The rest was, despite the occasional lapse into familiarity, exactly as it was "supposed" to be.

We chatted awkwardly on the couch—well, he chatted awkwardly, I made calm and smooth conversation. After all, I'd *done* this before.

Then, after one glass of wine, I reached forward and unlatched his belt. I slipped my hand inside and gently started rubbing. He was already hard, and he only got harder under the pressure of my hand. When he was completely stiff, I stood up and slowly pulled my shirt over my head. He sat, watching, like a dutiful pupil. I dropped it to the floor.

I began to dance slowly, twisting my hips from side to side, curving languorously in front of him, as I unhooked my bra and let it slip to the floor. Then my pants and my underwear. I was fully naked, except for my heels. He just stared.

I began unbuttoning his shirt, tugging off one arm and then another, sending my nails in red lines across his skin, grabbing and caressing the flesh. His shirt was on the floor. I slid first the condom, and then my body, onto his cock, which had never been so hard. I began to curve my body against his—one, two, three, four. One, two, three, four. Gradually picking up speed, squeezing my legs together, pushing him tightly inside, deeper, holding on to the back of the couch as I pulled myself further into and against him.

It didn't take long until his reserve (shyness?) broke, and he wrapped his arms around me and started pushing himself into me with a frenzy of desire. One, two, three…and—with a grip so tight I could barely breathe, he pressed me to him, and even though he was completely inside me, still I wanted more. I grab his head between my hands and press him to my chest.

"Lick me," I tell him.

And while he could barely muster the coordination as I'm

riding him like a bronco, he licked and bit my breasts, and I started to shudder as the sensation ran through my body. Grabbing my ass in his hands now, the fingers digging into my skin, spreading me wider, drawing me closer, my clitoris on fire, liquid oozing out of both of us, electricity shooting out of every contact, and all of my insides drawn to every part that could touch him, that could feel him, under my fingers, my thighs, my breasts, my legs, everything ultimately drawn to the fire between my legs while I strained to get him in deeper, to stuff him into me, as I groaned, and then his cock collapsed inside me, his body collapsing around me, and we exhaled the deep exhalation of release and satisfaction that is reserved for the completion of physically strenuous activities which fill you with dizzy pleasure.

I smiled to myself.

Waiting a minute for his breath to return before slowly disentangling myself and standing up, I kissed him lightly on the cheek.

"Thanks. That was wonderful."

He looked at me like a grateful dog. I kept this second smile to myself as I pulled my clothes back on.

"Won't you stay the night?" he asked.

I laughed lightly. "Sorry, dear, don't think you could afford it." And with that, and one more kiss, I made my way back downstairs to find a taxicab home.

* * *

I felt like I'd been given a rare opportunity and I should *really* be taking advantage of it—which is easier said than done. Okay, so I had an arrangement with an accommodating lover to fulfill any of my fantasies (within reason), and part of the deal was secrecy, so I should have been jumping up and down with euphoria at all those things I'd always wanted to do, and never had the nerve—or the companion.

But there's a reason why some of your fantasies stay in your head, relegated to the world of dreams or masturbation material—some of them just aren't realistic, and some of them are just embarrassing.

Still—I didn't know how long this arrangement would last, and he certainly seemed willing to accommodate my desires, so I figured I would push myself to concoct a scenario which I'd always dreamed of trying but never thought I actually would.

If he laughed, and it failed, or if he agreed, and it worked—no one else would know, and I'd have done it, or at least tried.

So I put my plans into motion. I made the date. I did the requisite shopping, made the requisite preparations, and held my breath.

We met first for drinks at a local bar. That was easy enough. We'd done *that* before. I wanted to wait until we'd both gotten a bit sloppy before making my confession. I could tell he was curious about the intention of the evening, but he held his tongue, as we occupied each other with our drinks and our kisses and our groping—but, oh, the groping was so careful, because I was keeping my cards close to my chest until we were both ready.

I decided we weren't ready at the bar. I waited until we got to the club, until after another round of vodka lemons, until we'd started to dance, until I could feel him start to press himself against me, and then, only then, did I pull him into a dark corner.

Only then did I take his hand and run it between my legs.

Only then did I let him feel me.

Only then did I let him discover what I was wearing strapped between my legs.

Only then did I let him realize I'd always fantasized

128

about being a boy.

His hand jumped a bit when it hit the hard plastic, but then he looked at me, I smiled at him, and we understood each other. He grinned, I grinned back, and then he felt me up. Just like a teenage girl would. Only I was the boy and he was the girl, as my hard plastic hung between my legs, securely fastened with my new leather harness, in a state of perpetual lust. As I ran my hand across his pants, I saw that we were not so different. He wasn't *just* a girl...

I leaned over and kissed him, and it was a kiss of such urgency, such depth, such desire, I felt myself falling into him, my knees weak, my pelvis unconsciously thrusting against his, his arms around my waist, and I lost myself in his mouth, in his warmth and heat, both of our bodies coming together against the wall of the club, swirling lights thankfully concealing more than they revealed.

We spent the rest of the night taking advantage of that darkness, rubbing against each other—groping, touching, stroking—on the dance floor and off. By the time we fell into the cab, on our way home, I felt as if I really had been hard for the past several hours, and I could tell by the dampness of my underwear that I was enjoying this as much as I thought I would.

Unfortunately, when we got back to his house, the combination of the brighter lights, the wearing off of the alcohol, and the unfamiliarity of the situation all combined to make us a bit nervous, a bit uncertain as to what should happen next. What should go where, exactly.

I was a little hesitant to take off my clothes, wondering what his reaction would be when seeing it made it all somehow more real (or, actually, when seeing it would remind us how artificial it really was). I didn't know how I'd react, either. I hadn't really looked at it on me, except the one time I'd tried the harness on in the store, and then, of course, when

I'd put it on that evening. Otherwise, I hadn't really looked, because I hadn't really wanted to see.

(While, in certain circles, there is something sexy about what I was wearing, at the same time, there is something fundamentally absurd and awkward about it, as well. I mean, it was *plastic*, after all.)

So what to do?

Well, we did what anyone else would have done—we dimmed the lights, had another glass of wine, and then I told him to get on the bed, on his stomach. The less eye contact, the better. I reached around and unzipped his pants, pulling them off and tossing them on to the floor. Even in my nervous state, I couldn't help but notice that he always did have a nice ass, although I'd never experienced it in quite this context…

Novice or not, I'd planned ahead enough to have lube on hand, and I nervously smeared some on the smooth hard surface.

He lay there, waiting. I listened to the sound of his breath, trying to gauge if it was nervous or excited or both. I couldn't tell.

When I felt like I was sufficiently slippery, I took a deep breath and stepped forward, my legs against the edge of the bed, the tip of the dildo just barely touching his ass.

I took another breath and gently ran my hands across his skin.

"Are you ready?" I asked.

"Uh huh," he replied. Nervous, definitely nervous.

I leaned forward and pushed. Just a little at first, and then a little more as his skin stretched, and he leaned back into me.

"Just relax," I said to him, although I could just as easily have been saying it to myself.

"Uh huh," he replied again, starting to breathe a bit more heavily.

"Does it hurt?" I asked, awkwardly frozen, uncertain how

130

to proceed.

"It's okay, just go slow."

Slow, indeed. Inch by inch, I slid in, and then out, in (a bit further), and then out (a bit further). As he started to moan, I could feel myself starting to get wet. I closed my eyes, and I could almost imagine that I felt his insides. I could almost imagine that it was me, in there, me feeling his warmth and his heat.

With my eyes closed, the sound of his breathing seemed to get louder, steadier. I could hear nothing else, except the quiet accompaniment of my own.

"Just relax," I said again, for my benefit and his, running my hands across his back, underneath to his stomach, pinching his nipples slightly, feeling the steady rise and fall of his chest, his lungs, beneath me, echoing the clenching I could feel around the dildo, trying to lose myself in the sensation, picking up speed as I sensed his readiness, slowing down when I felt his tension.

Once I felt like I'd made it all the way in, I sat there for a few seconds, letting the friction hold us both, and then I began to move. As if in affirmation, he reached around, grabbing my thigh.

"Is it too hard?" I asked, hoping he wouldn't ask me to slow down.

"No," he said, between heavy breaths, "it's fine. Don't stop."

That was all I had to hear. With my eyes closed, his breath and mine were the only sounds I could hear, I gave up all sensation in exchange for the pressure of his muscles and the movement of my pelvis. I couldn't feel the straps of the harness anymore, I couldn't feel my feet or my hands or the floor, as the dildo and I became united in our desire to go deeper and deeper.

Not content to be passive, my hand reached around his

waist again, searching for another toy on the other side of his body. I found it, and it was as hard as mine. I grinned. This was turning him on as much as me. I felt somehow vindicated. In the darkness, in the silence, in the space left between the heavy breathing, there was no room left for weirdness. All we felt was our desire and our need to move faster.

So move faster I did—my pelvis against his ass, my hand along his cock. There was no me left in the equation, no him. This was not an exercise of personalities. This was anonymous. This was need, pure and simple. This was desire. This was lust. This was both of us, bursting at the seams, desperate for relief.

I didn't want to look at him, I didn't want him to look at me. Neither of us was thinking of anything else but how to get deeper. How to move faster. How to maintain my grip on his cock, how to maintain my speed, while my hips kept moving, and the sweat was making everything slip, and I could feel my desire dripping down my legs, and thank god I'd put the harness on as tightly as I had, because there was no way it would have resisted all the lubrication—both natural and bottled.

The more I shoved, the more the other end of the dildo pressed against me, and I don't know if it was a lucky exercise of fate or a result of careful and strategic planning, but the other plastic end, the one not reserved for giving him pleasure, was giving it to me, right against my swelling and aching clitoris, and suddenly my speed and pressure weren't just about him, they were also about me.

We were both seeking satisfaction, and we were both running out of patience.

Bang, bang, bang. I stopped thinking about him. I stopped being careful. Luckily there was enough lubrication leaking everywhere, so I didn't seem to be hurting him—but unless he'd yelled really loud, I don't think I'd have been able to tell. I was completely lost in the moment, totally seduced by the fact that I was getting both of us off at the same time. It was hypnotic.

Hand, ass, pelvis, clit. Hand, ass, pelvis, clit. In, out, in, out, thrust, pull, thrust, pull, and then, and then, and then, coming, coming, coming—him, in a white mess all over my hand, me in a collapsing heap of falling stars against leather and plastic and everything very wet.

I stayed there for a moment or two, feeling my breath, feeling his breath, waiting for the world to slow down, for the ground to stabilize under my feet, to return to earth, and then, gingerly, tenderly, slowly, I began to withdraw.

"Is it okay?" I asked timidly, apparently my courage also dripping onto the bedclothes.

He just panted, and I took that for all the encouragement I needed. I took it slow, I kept taking it slow, rubbing my hands across his ass in what I imagined to be a soothing manner, until I was fully out, and then he slid facedown on the bed, and I slid on top of him.

I lay there, my dick between his legs the way his had been between mine so many times, his lungs lifting our bodies up and down, as we both fell asleep.

* * *

The fatal mistake happened later that week. High on the euphoria of our adventures, we got carried away and forgot Rule 5.

I'd been at a party when he called.

"Where are you? Are you at home?"

"Nope. I'm out with Rose. Why?"

"Why don't you stop by after? We're all at the International Bar. I think we'll be here for a while."

"Oh yeah?" I wasn't exactly sure how I felt about that.

"We're all" could mean a lot of different things. I didn't know if that was what I had in mind.

"Do come. It will be nice to see you."

Pause. I couldn't resist that combination of guilt and romance. "Okay. I'll stop by on my way home if it's not too late."

(But I knew how it would be. I knew it wouldn't be "too late." I knew that I wouldn't be able to keep hanging out with the girls, knowing that he was waiting for me, knowing that I'd said I'd stop by, and, of course, after another drink, I made my exit. I did kind of want to see him, I did want to find out what he had in mind, and I couldn't focus on what I was doing knowing that he was the next stop on my list, watching the clock, waiting for my arrival. So I betrayed my convictions and headed to the International.)

When I turned up, I saw, to my dismay, that they were "all" there. Kevin, Mia, Richard, Kelly, Patricia, and even a couple people I didn't know. He was there, right in the middle, in a haze of smoke and pot fumes. People all around, empty beer bottles in front. I sighed. I had a terrible feeling I'd done the wrong thing.

"Come on!" he exclaimed enthusiastically, throwing his arm around my shoulder and pulling me to him. "Have a drink!" A freshly opened Corona was thrust in my direction.

"I don't like beer," I said quietly, as I took it, knowing that if I held onto it for just a minute, I could put it back on the table where someone else would quickly claim it.

I didn't stay long, just long enough to be totally bored. Just long enough to remember why it hadn't worked when we'd tried to "combine" our lives. The only thing was how much I liked his body and how drawn him were to mine, the way we couldn't stop touching each other, the way we couldn't get enough—but when he threw our friends into the mix, when him tried to organize a night out, that's when we clashed.

"Where are you going?" he whispered drunkenly in my general direction.

With the calm of a sober individual in a group of punters, I replied, "I'm going home. I'm quite tired."

He grabbed my hand and pulled me to him. "No, don't. Come on. Stay. We'll go home together."

Everyone else was staring. They all still thought (quite intentionally) that we were still broken up. They were starting to whisper. This was not at all what I had in mind.

"Walk me out," I said, getting up from the table and heading for the door, slipping my hand out of his grip before he could realize what was happening. But he wasn't *so* drunk, and he certainly wasn't *so* stupid, and he followed me outside.

"Don't you want to stay?" he asked, hesitantly.

"No. I don't. It's too smoky, and I'm tired."

He stared at me for a second. I stared back at him. Despite his idiocies, he was still beautiful. Despite the fact that he occasionally tore me inside out, I still couldn't get his hooks out of my skin. Despite the fact that I was irritated at the whole situation, I still wanted to go home with him.

And he knew it.

"Wait," he said, spinning around and dashing back into the bar. He came back out fifteen seconds later, and thirty seconds later we were in a cab, heading to his place.

Even drunk, I knew he'd still be good in bed. And he was. And I enjoyed it. Despite the beer on his breath and the smell of cigarettes in the air, his limbs were still lean, his cock still perfect, and the touch of his tongue on my nipples still made them instantly hard, still sent ripples through my clitoris, still made me feel intoxicated by his very presence.

But then the next morning, when I woke up still tired, and heard him saying something about our new routine and how much he loved routines, I knew it would have to end. I didn't like routines. I didn't like the feeling of expectations and responsibility. And I knew that I didn't want another night in the bar with him. No more beer or reefer or conversation with his nice but totally boring friends. All I'd ever wanted was him, his flesh and his body and his limbs pounding against mine, but there was no realistic way to make that work, to isolate that from the rest of real life, so this was the end, of him and me, and of the arrangement.

But I knew that I had one more time left with him and, damn it, it was going to be a good one.

* * *

I rolled over onto my side.

"Kiss me," I said.

He rolled over to face me, and we each stared at each other for a moment before our faces came together, and his tongue into my mouth. I closed my eyes and let his tongue fill my mouth and my lips and my senses as my body ached for more of him, and I pulled myself closer, against his chest, and his shoulders, and his legs, and his cock. Almost accidentally, almost teasingly, I pressed my pelvis forward, letting him slip forward just enough to slide into the self-lubricated wetness of my outer lips.

I acted like I hadn't felt a thing, and we kept kissing, as his cock, slowly, began to push its head forward, searching for the entrance into my insides. Millimeter by millimeter, he pushed as I did not cooperate—at first. But then I couldn't stand it, I had to feel him, so I sent my hand down to wrap itself around the base of his cock and began to slowly move back and forth—not quite jerking him off, but enough to make his breath quicken, to make the skin tighten even more, and to tease that sensitive area just inside my pussy, along the circle of skin at the entrance, to make me moan and speed up my pace.

The thrusting of his pelvis grew more insistent, more aggressive, as he shoved his way incrementally inside me. I didn't have the strength to resist, and I spread my legs just an inch or two further apart to allow him all the way inside.

And when I say all the way, I mean, all the way.

I don't know what it was about his size or his shape, but every time he slid his way into me, for that first instant, I always marveled at how perfectly he fit, as though we were designed to sit inside each other, at how the tip of his cock pressed against my g-spot, at how the base and his balls pressed against the outer lips of my vagina, and everything in between fit everything in between.

Slowly, he shoved his way in and slid his way out. Once, twice, three times...and then he pulled all the way out.

"No," I moaned, my hands on his ass. "Come back in..."

"Where's the vibrator?" he asked.

"I don't know. I think it's in the drawer beside the bed."

"Get it. I want it."

"*You* want it?"

"Yes. You'll see. Get it."

I reached over and pulled the purple plastic vibrator out of the drawer.

"Okay. Now what?"

"Lie on your stomach. Put the vibrator underneath you. And use it."

"I don't want to masturbate now. I want you fuck me..."

He grinned at me. "Don't worry. I'll fuck you. Get on your stomach. You'll see."

"Alright. You're the boss."

I rolled over, lying on top of the vibrator, turning it on. I began to grind myself against it, sending waves of battery-powered stimulation through my clitoris. Startled, I felt him get on top of me, slipping his cock into my pussy.

"Oh my god," I moaned. It felt incredible.

He didn't answer. Every answer I needed, I could hear in his breath.

"Can you feel it?" I asked.

"You have no idea," he replied, as his thrusts grew deeper and faster.

The vibrations went through me, through my clitoris, through my pussy, and through his cock. It was like we were hooked up to the same power generator. Pushing, pushing, pushing, my pelvis pushed back, his pelvis pushed forward, his cock slipping in and out of my pussy which I knew was leaking onto the bed…my clitoris throbbing, I reached around with my other hand and grabbed his waist, pressing him closer to me, pressing my pelvis even further up. I wanted him to split me in two.

I could feel his heat between my legs, inside my cunt, against my ass, mixing with the insistent whirring heat of the vibrator's double A batteries. My clitoris was huge against the plastic, the opening of my vagina huge against the base of his cock, his swollen balls slapping against me, as his speed grew faster and the vibrations rocked both of us.

He was in deep, but not deep enough, because he pushed so far in, I felt like he was hitting my uterus, my stomach, my lungs, all the way through, really splitting me in two with the size of him, with the swollen heat of him.

I began to moan, he began to moan, the vibrator whirring beneath everything, all of us together, shameless, aching, so full of desire and ready to burst, bed rocking against the wall, all ordinary everyday togetherness abandoned in this moment of animal lust and sweat and need.

As though waiting for my sign, once the double A's started sending their signal straight the pressure point of my clitoris, and I began to inhale rapidly, with my usual string of, "oh my god, oh my god, oh my god," his pace doubled, and we both came together, a mess of electrical vibrations and human quiverings, his cum inside me, my wetness all over the bed, until we were silent, left only with the sound of our breath and the quiet whirring of the vibrator.

Reluctant to break the moment, but irritated with the almost painful heat it was sending through my insides, I reached down to turn it off.

As I did so, he rolled off me and onto his side.

"That was the last time, wasn't it?" he asked.

"What do you mean?" I replied, confused.

"It'll never be so good again, will it?"

I smiled at him, his face glistening with sweat, little bits of moisture even clinging to his eyelashes. I wiped my finger along his forehead.

"Who knows?" I said, as we grinned at each other.

The Game

I wasn't trying to play a game. I swear it wasn't like that at all. I mean, was it my fault that I wanted you? Was it my fault that I wanted you, with your clothes off, in my bed? That I couldn't look at you without imagining how your arms would look after I'd ripped your shirt off? That I saw your legs and remembered what they were like wrapped around my body? Seeing you with your clothes on, frankly, seemed to make it all that much more intense because it just sent my brain spinning through fantasies of what I couldn't get, what I didn't want to wait for, and it made a mockery of our civil (fully-clothed) conversations, because while we pretended so hard to be adults, I wanted anything but.

I wanted you, but you wanted her.

I remember the way you told me. We were on the couch, having one of our civil conversations while I was having one of my fantasies, and I'd just finished telling you about who I'd kissed while on holiday (all the while thinking about in whose mouth I'd really like to find myself inside and wondering if you could read my mind), and then you told me about who you'd kissed on your last business trip (and I figured that meant you couldn't, unless this was the game you were playing), and I tried to pretend that I didn't care (since, after all, fully clothed and civil, why should I?), yet all the while I wondered how many smiles I'd have to fake, how tight I'd have to keep my legs crossed, and if I needed to sit on my hands to keep from doing something I might regret.

I didn't sit on my hands, but I still managed to keep them to myself, even after you told me that you kept thinking about me the whole time I was away (whatever that meant), even

141

while you put your arm around me as I put my shoes on (whatever that meant), and even after you kissed me goodbye with a hunger verging on desperation (whatever that meant).

I left before I'd do something I might regret.

I left because you told me you were in love with her.

With her. Not with me.

I play by the rules. I don't play games. If you wanted her, you should have her. I wasn't going to get in the way. I wasn't going to interfere. Why should I? If you didn't want me, why should I want you?

But I couldn't kick you out of my head as thoroughly as you'd kicked me out of your life (that goodbye kiss notwithstanding), and so you continued to invade my thoughts and my fantasies. I'd wake up in the morning dreaming of the way your tongue tasted in my mouth, and I'd fall asleep dreaming of the way your teeth bit my breast. I'd lose track of points during meetings because I couldn't stop thinking how you felt when you'd fucked me from behind, and I wouldn't notice how my food tasted because I was too lost in the memory of how you kissed my spine.

Everything felt perfect when you were on my mind, until I remembered that she was on yours.

Part of me (the sensible part) told me to walk away. To leave her to you and you to her. The other part (the naughty part) told me—well, it didn't tell me anything, it just desired you. It lusted for you. It longed for you. For your nails on my back and your tongue in my mouth and your arms crushing me close.

I didn't know how to reconcile them, what with the completely contradictory mixed messages. I ran my batteries down trying to distract myself, but it's funny how, even though fantasies are better than real life, they always remain remarkably empty, remarkably flat, like the sheerest, most exquisite diaphanous fabric that does no good at sheltering you from any real cold.

I wanted you, and I wanted your warmth, and I drove myself crazy longing for you and yet trying everything I could to convince myself that I didn't care.

What was worse? The lies or the unfulfilled desire?

So I decided to give myself a present. It wasn't a game. It wouldn't continue. It would be one precious gift to fill my aching need, to quench my thirsty fantasies, and then I would walk away.

But first I needed that gift to myself. I needed you, one more time.

I didn't know what was happening between you and the girl, because you never mentioned her again, but I could pretend not to care as long as I got my last turn. As long as I could have one more hedonistic hour to spend in your arms.

You'd invited me over for dinner (a peace offering? a sign of guilt? a gesture of affection?), and I decided that would be my opportunity.

I wore a dress I knew you wouldn't be able to resist. I wore the heels that always got me my way. And I kissed you the second I walked through the door. The days (weeks? months?) of hunger came rushing to the surface as I pushed you against the wall and myself against you. The girl (whoever she was) didn't stand a chance.

You pressed your tongue inside my mouth, your days (weeks? months?) of hunger also rushing to the surface, as we clung to each other in the hallway. We had yet to utter a single word, but we'd communicated more than in all those civil conversations. All those hours of (fully clothed) adult interaction evaporated into a blink of bullshit and all that was real left the energy charged with something so potent it could never fit into one of your run-on sentences or one of my introspective analyses.

This was real. This was hot. And I wanted more.

Without saying anything, you pulled my dress over my head and ran your hands over my hips. I leaned back against the wall, arching my spine, as your tongue licked my stomach and my breasts, and I grabbed your hair in my fists. You shoved me hard against the wall, and I wrapped my legs around your waist, my arms around your shoulders, and you let your pants fall to the floor while we shoved ourselves into each other's mouths.

I was the first to say anything.

"One more time. Can I have you one more time?"

You grinned at me, and I couldn't tell if you were grinning at my words or my actions or at the simple fact of my desire.

At this point, I didn't care. I seized the opportunity to grab your lip between my teeth and to pull you even closer to me, to tighten the grip of my legs around your waist and to beg you to fuck me.

Which you did, of course, and you did it as superbly as I remembered, or, actually, it might have been even better, because it was so what I wanted and needed that it felt so perfect to feel your breath on my face and your hands on my ass, while my legs stayed clenched around your waist.

I was conscious of nothing but the feeling of you upon my skin, receiving every message through a code of direct sensation. It was not the force of your body against mine that made me stop breathing, it was the fact that it was your body, that you were inside me and around me as though I belonged to you. It may have only been a moment of physical pleasure, but it said everything we'd never been able to speak with our mouths. The moment contained every bit of language we had lost or never found, but all I was knew was the way you felt inside me, between my legs, my body against yours.

We were pressed against each other, and I was against the wall, without any space to breathe or move, but why would I have wanted to do either? I'd been waiting for this moment, to feel as much of your skin against every inch of mine, and I wasn't going to compromise for a second.

My legs in sharp angles to your hips, holding me up as I clung to your neck and shoulders, marveling at how beautiful your body was as though I'd never seen it before, as though I hadn't woken up next to you time and time again, as though everything were happening for the first time, while I hoped it would never end.

You couldn't have been pressed further inside of me, and if it weren't for the sweat making us slippery, we might have fused ourselves together. Somehow, despite the apparent precariousness of our position, it felt perfect to me, and, if your moans were any evidence, it worked for you, as well. You pushed and pushed, harder and harder, pressing me so hard against the wall, I started to wonder if it would cave in. I kept my hands clutched around you while you thrust yourself inside me and I thrust myself against you, your cock filling up my insides as I curved my body to allow you to go as deep as possible, as I curved my body to echo your curves, as I curved my body to fuse myself into you.

"You can't wear this dress around me," you panted in my ear.

"What? Why not?" I asked, barely able to get the words out as you repeatedly, rhythmically, pounded me against the wall.

"Because it makes your ass look too damn good."

I laughed. Just the kind of thing you would say. I angled my clenched legs down, around your ass, forcing you so close, like a huge pair of pincers, so that you had to stop moving and just try to catch your breathe, sweat glistening on your face.

You looked at me, waiting to see what I had to say.

"Since it's our last time, I want to do it how I like it. From behind."

You grinned.

"Of course."

And then, without a moment's hesitation, you'd thrown me down on the bed, my dress still around my waist, and us in my favorite position—me on hands and knees against your pillows, your arms on my waist, your cock between my legs, and my finger on my clitoris.

This was the moment of my fantasy.

I felt you thrusting in a rhythm which started off slow but picked up pace as though you were somehow synced up with my finger which was going round and round in circles as my clitoris swelled and your cock swelled, and the sweat dripped off both of us, and I could barely breathe because I didn't want to do anything to spoil the moment, while I felt the orgasm hovering on the edges of my consciousness, but I didn't want to come until you did, and so I tried to keep myself in teasing limbo while feeling your quickening pace. You got faster, I got faster, while my orgasm came closer and closer and you went deeper and deeper, and then I couldn't stand it anymore. With my eyes closed, I let go.

The waves started slow, at my fingers and toes, enveloping me with the kind of attack every surfer fears, where you're drowning in the water, and it's rushing over your head with no end in sight, and you can't breathe because you can't find enough oxygen to inhale, and you certainly can't even tell which part of your body goes where, and, for that moment, we really were fused in two, and I never wanted it to end, and I didn't want to think that this was the last time, because this was what I'd wanted all along.

As my consciousness returned, I gradually became able to tell which parts of your body were intertwined with mine, and how. I started to register every sensation, every moment, for the infinite log of my imagination. She could have you for the rest of her life, but I had had this moment, which I would make sure never to forget—and could she honestly say the same? Had she paid enough attention to remember how fine and blonde the hairs on your arm were? Had she bothered to notice the muscular lines of your thighs or the creamy white of your hands or the exact shape of your eyelashes against the precise blue of your eyes?

I'd had the fantasies, I'd had the real thing, and now, somehow, I'd had managed to combine the two. For this instant and forever in my mind, I had you just where I wanted you—right between my legs.

DAHLIA SCHWEITZER

The First Fantasy

Hey, listen, I've never written a fantasy about a girl before, but ever since our conversation, I can't keep thinking about what I want to do with you. I've got this idea in my head that we're going to go out, and we get all dressed up, like you said you like to do (and like I like to do, too), and you're wearing a suit, because I bet you look HOT in a suit, and I'm wearing some dress with a short skirt so that you can grab my ass with the utmost of ease, and because I'm secretly hoping that, at some point later in the night, you'll put your hand on my thigh, like a junior high boy hoping to cop a feel, and of course, my thigh has to be naked and exposed, or that's not as much fun, and then my skin is there, under your hand, and I don't know what you're feeling, but everything is tingling for me, and then you'd slowly inch your way up my thigh—we must be sitting down somewhere—and you're going up my thigh, and I'm totally dying, and, oh wait, I forgot the best part...

So before we go out, I've already told you that I want you to wear a strap-on, under your pants, because I want to fuck a girl wearing a strap-on, because I've got this fantasy about fingering you and giving you head at the same time, and I keep seeing in my head what you'd look like, with your head against the wall, and your nipples getting hard against your shirt, and I've got your plastic cock in my mouth, and my finger is sort of underneath or behind it, so that I can slip it in and out, and you're breathing hard, and I'm going faster, but not too fast because you feel so good that it feels like a waste to go too fast, but I love feeling you contract around me, and feeling you getting wetter and wetter around me, and then you

149

pull me up, and you zip yourself closed and you drag me into the bathroom, and then you lift my skirt up and tug my panties to the floor, and then you drop your pants, and your hard plastic cock is there and you start to fuck me against the wall of the bathroom, and I laugh to myself because we're two girls in the girls room, so we're not breaking any rules, and you ask me why I'm laughing, but I don't tell you, because as soon as I hear your voice, I remember the million reasons why you turn me on, and I start to kiss you, and you're fingering my clitoris as you're fucking me and it's totally the best sex I've ever had and I can't stop touching your nipples which are so hard and red that I have to put them in my mouth and I'm licking them and sucking on them and you're still fucking me, but I don't want to come, I'm not ready to come, so I step back, making you come out of me, and then I ask if I can go down on you.

You laugh. You ask me if you could ever say no to a question like that. I laugh back, because I can't imagine ever not wanting to go down on you, but I don't tell you that, because I'm shy, and I don't know what you think of me, but I do know that I want to taste you really, really badly, so we loosen your harness just enough so I can shove it aside and then I get down on my knees, and I press your lips apart with my left hand, and then I start by just running my fingers back and forth because I can't believe how wet and swollen you are, and I can't believe that you are so wet and swollen because of me, and then I start to lick, even while my fingers are still there, and I'm running my finger in circles around your clitoris and my tongue is going back and forth, almost lapping, like an animal, and it amazes me how much I feel like an animal.

I know that sex is supposed to be primal, but it's never made me feel like an animal before. It's just always felt like something "adults do," and even when it's good, it just always made me feel somehow like a grownup, but something about you makes me feel like a dog, but a dog in all the good ways.

Okay, maybe not like a dog, but like a tiger, and I want to get dirty with you, and to get messy with you, and do all the things that adults don't do—or maybe they do, I just don't read the right magazines?

And so I'm licking you in this bathroom, and I'm fingering you in this bathroom, and there is something so completely hot about the fact that you've got this fake plastic cock, and it's just dangling off to one side, and you've got a clitoris, as well, and I've got my fingers and my tongue all up inside you, and it feels like you're just oozing sex, and I can feel myself getting wet, even though I'm still kneeling on the floor so you can reach me, and I take my left hand and start fingering myself while I'm fingering you, and I don't know who starts to come first, because it's almost like our bodies are talking to each other, like we're tapped into the same frequency, and I can feel first your hips start to move and your legs start to tighten, and then I feel my clitoris start to get really, really swollen, and then you're breathing harder, and then I'm breathing faster, and I can feel your muscles starting to quiver underneath my finger, and my tongue moves faster, and I want you to come because I want to know what it feels like underneath my tongue, and the thought of tasting you come makes me start to come, and I can barely concentrate on all the things I'm doing, and I'm starting to come, and it takes every ounce of concentration not to stop licking you and touching you, but as soon as I start to come, you start to come, and thank god, because I can barely keep it all together, and then you're dripping onto me, and I'm dripping onto the floor, and I stop everything and lean my head against your stomach, and just feel myself quivering and feel you quivering against my fingers, and I can taste you in my mouth, and it's just total sensory overload.

Then you pull me up, and we're kissing, and it's not like it is sometimes, after sex, where you're kind of spent and exhausted, but somehow it's even hotter and more intense because it was so good that both of us just want more, and we're kissing in the bathroom, but people want to get in, so they're knocking on the door, and we laugh at each other, and then I dress you up again, adjusting all the necessary straps and buttons and zippers, and then I grab your hand and pull you out onto the dance floor, and we dance together until we're the last ones on the dance floor, and then I bring you home, and we do it all over again.

Post-Paula

Paula had been my one great love, in the way that someone with whom you have had an obsessive co-dependent relationship is a great love. You live intertwined in the magic of someone else (I'd say in the magic of someone else's *life* except that it isn't really their life anymore, just as much as yours stops being only yours in those fused-at-the-hip relationships)—until, suddenly, they are gone, and you realize that maybe it wasn't the best relationship in the world, and you'd do it differently next time, but the main problem is that you can't imagine who else you'd do it differently *with.*

Because, obviously, you've lived a combined life with this person for ten years, where they were The One, the end and the beginning and the middle, and you can't imagine your life without them, and you can't imagine how it will be now that you can't even meet for lunch or call them after bad conversations with your mother.

I'm not going to say that breakups after years of co-dependency are always bad, because that's not fair, but breakups after co-dependency are *usually* bad, especially when she is sleeping with Jason now, and I'm still sleeping alone.

Not a pretty picture, now is it?

One on hand, you've got a middle-aged man who has seen better days (in some people's perspectives, like Paula's) or who might just be getting started (in other people's more positive perspectives, like my therapist's)…

And you've got a girl, as charming as ever who looks at least ten years younger than her actual age, and perhaps all the more charming to me now for her unavailability…

Who do *you* think comes out looking better?

I stare the answer in the face every morning.

Paula didn't want to see me, for lunch or anything, and, frankly, I didn't want to see her, because when I did, I couldn't help begging her to take me back, and she couldn't help crying and saying she might, and then every next day, without fail, I'd get a terse but polite email from her telling me that it had been a mistake, and she was quite happy with Jason, thank you, and weren't we better off without each other, anyway?

I was having a hard enough time tying my shoes in the morning, I didn't think I could handle anymore of those rollercoaster episodes—which is why I told my friends to forget it every time they started with their "Mark, I think I know someone you should meet."

Love. Forget it. I'd seen the damage it could cause, and I wasn't coming back for more. I figured middle-aged men were single all the time. I could pick up golf.

They kept trying, though, and I kept resisting. I didn't want to meet anyone. I didn't want the "does she like me?" I didn't want the "I like her, but she won't return my phone calls." I didn't want to think about anyone else. I didn't want to worry about anyone else. My self-esteem couldn't handle it. If one more feminine heel stepped on my ego, I didn't think I'd ever recover. At least golf clubs were consistent.

So imagine my dismay when I met Erika.

Erika had just moved to New York. She knew my friends Rachel and Linda, who'd actually been raving to me about her even before she'd come to town, but I'd ignored their efforts for all the expected reasons. Then, one night, there we were at Local 138, when this woman walked in. Almost six feet, curly red hair down her back, wide blue eyes, perfect skin, lips—the kind of woman you'd expect to see on the cover of *Vogue* before you saw her walking down Stanton.

Only she wasn't one of those model types. She wasn't drinking Cosmopolitans. She wasn't dangling a cigarette between long, immaculate fingers. She looked great, but not in that overly trendy way, where you know either the woman got her look from a magazine or the magazine got their look from her.

I was transfixed.

Rachel and Linda clearly noticed, because they kept making extended trips to the bar—together—leaving me to make awkward conversation while trying not to stare.

I couldn't believe it. My mindfully anxious inner voice kept shouting that this was a bad idea, but that part of me seemed to shrink the more we talked and the more I drank. A couple other friends turned up, and soon it was a group, but I still had eyes only for her, and all my friends seemed to find this incredibly entertaining, but luckily enough Pilsners, and this woman's eyes, made me blissfully oblivious to their meaningful glances.

We'd started drinking early, so even though it was only around midnight by this point, we were all a bit sloppy, which added a nice air of warmth and informality to the proceedings.

Being as it was the end of June, conversation soon turned to summer weekends, and where we were all spending the three-day weekend that came along with this year's Fourth of July.

As always, the Hamptons were a popular favorite. The occasional upstate New York destination. The Jersey Shore. Staying in the city and Central Park.

And for me, the annual tradition of David's Long Island home. I'd been going there for as long as I could remember, ever since I'd met David my freshman year at NYU. He'd ended up moving back to Long Island after graduation, marrying his high school sweetheart, and settling down to a profitable and rewarding career as an editor and husband. I'd remained in the city, choosing ten years of a co-dependent relationship and an attempted career as a video game designer, but at least I still got my yearly invitation.

As for Erika, and her first Fourth of July in New York, she hadn't even thought about what to do.

We all blinked at each other, and the rush of invitations came. "Come to Montauk!" "To Ocean Grove!" "Milton!" Etc. I couldn't help it, everyone was jumping all over everyone else with overeager, alcoholically-lubricated hospitality, so I didn't think twice. "Long Island!"

She turned. She smiled. She looked at me. "Okay, sure, that would be great. Thanks."

Everyone stopped, mouths caught in mid-motion. They slowly turned their heads to stare at me to see how I would respond.

"Uh, yeah, okay," I said, trying to make the words sound easy. "We'll do it."

"Great." She beamed at me.

Everything paused and then, with a sudden burst of noise worthy of a conductor's upswing, conversation resumed apace.

As though nothing had happened.

As though nothing out of the ordinary had occurred.

As though everything was normal.

I smiled and nodded along with the rest of them while my brain was reeling. What kind of mess had I gotten myself into? It wasn't that I didn't like her, because I *did*, but a weekend? Away? Out of town? At David's? I barely *knew* her. Did this mean she was interested? Did this mean she was interested in *me*—or Long Island? The questions (or maybe it was just the alcohol) made me dizzy, but she was a smart girl, my Erika. It didn't take long until she'd cornered me at the bar.

"Hey, I just wanted to make sure it was okay about the fourth?" she asked, nervously, peering at me with her blue gray eyes, rimmed with a darker blue.

I tried not to fall over. I just stared at her, leaning against the bar, in a comfortably masculine fashion, and held my drink for support.

"Yes, sure, it's fine." If I spoke slowly and remembered to breathe, maybe I wouldn't stutter. "It's just that, well, uh, the house isn't so big, so we're probably going to end up staying in the same room."

I would have given her a dashingly contrite Hugh Grant smile, but that was completely impossible in my state of mind, so I just ended up wincing apologetically.

She smiled hesitantly. "Look, Mark, I would totally love to go, but only if it's okay with you. I really don't want to give you a stressful weekend, but I think it would be nice."

"Are you sure?"

"Yes." She placed her hand on my arm reassuringly. "I think David's place in Long Island sounds lovely. I really do. I'd like to come."

"Really?" I asked, starting to feel a bit better about things, although I couldn't think why, because I was still in the midst of the situation.

"Great!" she said, grinning. "Now can I buy you a drink?"

* * *

The drive up was uneventful and provided no answers to my unrelenting questions. I kept stealing glimpses at her while I drove, trying to figure out what was going through her head. The woman's face was inscrutable. I was driving out to Long Island with the Sphinx—only a hotter, sexier version. She chatted a bit in the car, enough to be pleasant but not enough to appear interested. She laughed at my jokes, enough to be convivial but not enough to appear besotted. I hadn't a clue if she had any ulterior motives, or, if she did, what they were. The worst part was, I couldn't decide if I wanted her to have ulterior motives. Maybe it would be nice to have a new platonic friend to take to the movies.

But no matter, it was nice having the company. It was nice being able to glance over to see her tapping her foot on the dashboard or fiddling with the radio or looking over at me. It had been a while since I'd driven with someone, much less a pretty girl, and no matter what her reasons for occupying my passenger seat, I liked having her there.

By the time we arrived at David's, despite whatever reservations I'd had, it was as though we'd been making this trip every year of our lives. We went swimming, took a couple long walks, loitering in fields and drinking tea in the shade like the perfect foursome. We helped David move some things out of his barn, had scotch by the pool, chattering all the while about everything from books and movies to politics and philosophy—while I started feeling like more and more of an idiot because I couldn't bring myself to hold her hand, and because I couldn't tell if that was what she wanted from me, anyway.

I knew if I didn't do something before bedtime (if that's what she wanted), it was going to be pretty damn awkward when we were alone together. And if I did something, either before or at bedtime, and that wasn't what she wanted, it might be even more awkward.

I watched the sky getting darker, a clock ticking down inside my head.

The later it got, the more nervous I felt.

The later it got, the more of an idiot I felt.

The later it got, the more I thought I had to do something and the more helpless I felt.

The ticking clock was the countdown to the death of my reputation.

158

I just couldn't bring myself, especially in front of David and Leigh, to act with their air of careless comfort. I felt fourteen all over again. I could hardly talk. I was a wreck.

Then, somehow, through no engineering on my part, Erika and I ended up alone in the kitchen, I with the responsibility of fetching barbeque sauce, her with the responsibility of finding tomatoes.

I figured it was now or really bad later, so I tried to kiss her against the refrigerator.

"No."

That word was all I needed to hear. I felt awful. I'd been nothing if not perfectly charming and gentlemanly, there hadn't been anything to set her off. It was obvious that she just didn't like me. I stammered an apology, some sort of explanation about mixed signals and misunderstandings, but before I could even figure out exactly what I was saying, she took her index finger and placed it square over my mouth.

"Shh."

I blinked and stopped trying to talk.

She smiled.

"We only met two days ago. I need to get to know someone a bit more before I do something like that…"

I began to apologize again. She pressed her finger harder, closing my mouth.

"Do you think you can wait another two hours? That should be about all I need."

I started to talk but then realized I didn't know what to say.

She smiled yet again, removing the finger. "Let's go bring this stuff out to David before he sends out the rescue committee, okay?"

And with that, she was on her way out the door and across the lawn, glancing at me over her shoulder. I swear I saw her wink.

* * *

I was a wreck of an entirely different sort all through dinner. Erika and I suddenly had a secret, and keeping it to ourselves was half the fun. Everything became conspiratorial. If there'd been sexual tension before, now it was tangible enough to have been the fifth member of our dinner party. It took all I had to remember to direct my conversation at David and Leigh, and not just to stare at Erika with my mouth open, while she took every opportunity to wink and smirk in my direction and to steal lingering touches on my thigh or arm every chance she could.

Dinner felt endless but not as endless as everything that came after—the girly conversation between Leigh and Erika as they cleared the table, and David and I cleaned the grill, the one last drink that became just-one-more last drink, the invitations for a video or a walk in the field which had to be politely deflected, the seemingly endless arrangements and goodnights and extra blankets that had to be executed and delivered before, finally, somehow I was closing the door to the room, and Erika was sitting on the bed, staring at me, and then it all felt hopelessly sudden.

I let the door latch quietly behind me, as I leaned against it and looked at her looking at me.

"Why don't you come over here?" she said, patting the space next to her on the bed.

That seemed like a good start. I walked over hesitantly and sat down.

"I think it's been way more than two hours." She smiled at me.

"Two hours?" I asked, confused.

"Still want to kiss me now?"

I got it. I leaned over and kissed her hard, on the lips. She kissed me back, her tongue slipping into my mouth as her hands slipped around my back and underneath my shirt. Her fingers were against my skin, her nails tracing patterns while she pressed me closer towards her. We fell over onto the bed, my body on top of hers, her legs wrapped around mine. I could feel myself pressing hard against her, and she must have been able to feel me, too, because she pressed against me, in response. I worried, for a second, that I might come before anyone had even taken their clothes off, but, as though she could read my mind, Erika started unbuttoning my shirt.

I slipped her out of her dress and dropped it on the floor beside my pants. She was wearing a black bra and the smallest pair of black satin underwear I'd ever seen in my life. Even though it was black, I could tell it was wet. I ran my fingers across the stained part, and she inhaled sharply.

"Can I?" I asked, tugging on the fabric.

"Please," she said, her eyes closed, hands spread flat against the bedspread.

I slowly slid one hand up her thigh and slipped them off, dropping them onto the pile. Using both my hands, I gently pushed her legs apart and lay down between them, running my tongue across her thigh and between her legs. She tasted sweet and clean, warm and wet. I licked slowly at first, in long gestures, from top to bottom, and then gradually added speed and pressure in circles around her clitoris while I carefully slipped first my index finger, and then my middle finger, inside her. While my tongue kept up its constant circles, my fingers pushed in and out, arched against the front of her pelvis, and she curved against me.

Reaching down, I pulled my underwear off and added it to the clothes on the floor. I was just leaning over to the table by the bed, to get the condoms that I knew stayed there for just these kinds of eventualities, when—

"Mark."

161

I froze and glanced over at her. Had I fucked up again?

"I don't want to have sex."

I knew it. I knew it. What could I say to recover?

"That's okay. That's fine. We don't need to. I'm sorry, I didn't mean to assume, we can just—"

She cut me off. "Do you mind just lying next to me?"

"Of course, of course."

As quick as a nine year old caught with his hand in the cookie jar, I slid down onto the bed and lay obediently beside her, trying to slow my pounding heart and wishing I could disappear.

We lay next to each other, quiet in the moment. Her breathing, me trying not to, in hopes that that might help me disappear.

Suddenly, I felt her fingers stroke the top of my hand, across my palm, fingers interlacing with mine, and then she was gripping my hand.

I slowly let myself return to breathing.

"Mark?"

"Yes?"

"I know it seems so hopelessly old-fashioned, but I think sex is always better when, you know, you know each other, you know?"

She went quiet. I squeezed her hand again, waiting to see if she had anything more to say.

It appeared as though she didn't.

I told her I agreed. I told her about Paula. I told her about my lack of love, about staying alone because you can't face the fear of having to learn to be alone again, and about how she'd been the first person since all this to make me want to risk myself once more.

And then it was her turn to squeeze my hand reassuringly, before turning over and kissing me long and hard. I wrapped my arms around her, holding her close, and

162

realizing that, in a way, I felt closer to her than if I'd been inside her, and yet, as the pressure between my legs indicated, I still ached to be there, too.

I shifted my hips back, hoping she hadn't noticed. The last thing I wanted to do was ruin the mood, making her feel I somehow hadn't been paying attention to a word she said, that I was just another dick-driven guy.

But she had noticed. She smiled at me, and ran her finger along my jaw, down my neck, across my chest, and between my legs. She took hold of me with her hands and gently started to rub.

I started to stammer something about how she didn't have to, about how it was okay, and something else that was incoherent, but she cut me off again, as she appeared to have a way of doing.

"Shh. Mark. It's okay. I said I didn't want to have sex. I'd still love to make you come."

Before I realized what was going on, she was between my legs, her mouth on my cock, her hands on my thighs, moving up and down, slowly, firmly, quickly, lightly—and just when the sensation got to be too much, when I felt the pressure building, she would stop and breathe lightly on the wet skin, running her tongue up the shaft, flicking the top, and I would moan, the blood pulsing, and then she'd be back on, shoving me inside her so far I would have worried about her throat if I was capable of thinking about anything other than willing her not to stop, oh god, not to stop—and then I noticed that her touch had relaxed, somehow, her rhythm slacked, one of her hands missing from my thigh while the other hand had stopped moving, and I opened my eyes, and looked down my body to see what had happened to hers.

She must have sensed my movement.

"Oh, sorry," she panted, "I'm just, I'm just about—"

And with that she moaned and shuddered and, maybe it

was my imagination, but I swear I felt wetness drip onto my leg and she shuddered again, and then smiled hugely at me, before pulling her right hand back out from between her legs, and wrapped it back around my cock.

It didn't take long after that.

With the combination of hand and tongue and lips and mouth, I could feel the pressure build in about thirty seconds, and then I came in her mouth, the delicious warmth mixing with the delicious intimacy, and I pulled her up beside me, and we kissed again and again and again.

I felt like I could never get enough.

And then, for the first time in a long time, I fell asleep next to someone else, holding them and letting them hold me.

What If

We've broken up. I *know* we've broken up. That isn't the issue. I was relieved we decided to end it—we are definitely better off apart. There is no question that you bring out the worst in me, and everything I represent terrifies you, despite your attempts to deny it.

But I still can't get you out of my head.

The sex has always been good between us, although I always felt like it could have been better—which, to be honest, is the best way to feel, because knowing that you are inching closer to something amazing keeps you hungry for more. Which also means that ever since we broke up, I can't stop thinking about you and me, together. Because I want more.

I don't care about the boyfriend stuff. The relationship routine, the dinners, the dates, the conversations and mutual schedule coordination—those can go to hell for all I care. I associate them with the annoyances and insecurities that went along with our brief affair. But the sex? Oh god, I want more.

I've been struggling with this letter in my head for weeks. It seems so absurd to write it to you. But I can't stop thinking about all the things I want to do to you, and all the things I want you to do to me.

Do you remember that time we lay on your couch and watched a movie, and I made you pause it so that I could drag you upstairs to let you fuck me? I keep running that scene through my head, and I keep thinking about all the things we could have done on that couch before going upstairs to bed.

I dream about lying on that couch beside you, stretched out along your body, my legs and arms draped over you even

165

though the couch was so big, we didn't have to share so much space. We're lying like that, watching the television (not each other), and we're following the movie like we're supposed to, and then I realize that my arm is resting against your crotch, and, even though you haven't moved at all, I can feel you getting hard against me.

All notions of plot evaporate as the movie instantly loses my attention, and I become engrossed in how subtly I can move my arm before you notice what I'm doing. It doesn't take long until you do, and then you tilt my head up, look me in the eyes, and ask in that ever-so-correct-but-still-wry manner I used to adore (but now find annoying), "What do you think you're doing?"

I'd smile, of course, and use the opportunity to unzip your pants and reach my hands into your underwear.

In my fantasy world, which, since it's a fantasy, doesn't follow the standard rules of time and space, I go down on you for a bit, and then, somehow, we're in your kitchen, and it's a different day and a different scene.

(Not that we ever did it in your kitchen, because you're too uptight for that, but in my world, anything goes.)

So we're in your kitchen, and I'm against the stove. Maybe I'm cooking or something? Who cares. Anyway, you're astonishingly aggressive, and you come up behind me and you pull my skirt up and my underwear down, and before I realize what's going on, I've already figured out that you're not wearing any pants, because your cock is shoved inside me and it's all I can do not to fall against the stove, because you're fucking me so hard, and I'm pressed up against you, and you're grabbing my breasts from behind, and I can't get over how good it feels, but it's still not what I want, so I turn around—

And now there's another abrupt scene cut, like flipping channels or something, and we've come back to your flat after a night at some bar, and in this dream, we are broken up, but we're kind of drunk, so we start groping at each other, and I take your pants off, and I go down on you, and you're leaning against the wall of your hallway, because we haven't even made it into your living room or bedroom or anywhere that could be called a room, and I've got you in my mouth, and I've forgotten how good you taste, because it's been months, and you've clearly forgotten how good I am, because you're moaning, and then I realize what's going on, and I remember that you're the one that broke up with me, and I stand up, and I look you in the eyes, and I ask you if you are still glad you gave me up.

You try to regain some sense of dignity and self-control, but you can't because I've wrapped my hand around your cock, and I'm moving just slow enough to distract most of your brain, but way too slow for you to think about coming, and I ask you again.

You swallow and you try to say something, but I pick up speed just a little bit, and then I go back down, putting you in my mouth, and I move back and forth several times, just enough to get you totally hard and totally slick, and then I stand back up, and I tell you that I'm going to go home.

(Because you gave me up.)

And then, with more force and passion than you ever showed me when we were together, you push me hard against the wall, and you shove my dress up until it's at my waist, and you barely even wait to pull my underwear to my knees, and then you've got yourself inside me, and you are holding my arms together above my head, and you've got a look of such hunger in your eyes that it almost terrifies me even while I realize it's what I've been waiting for all along.

You're so hard and so hot that it doesn't take you long to come, and it's a moment that seems to be over before it actually happened because you only take a single deep exhale, and then you pull yourself out in order to pick me up, and you carry me into your bedroom and drop me onto the bed.

Standing there, like a conquering hero, you look at me, spread out on the bed, palms flat along the sheet, legs open, dress still awkwardly along my waist, and then you pull the top part of it down, so it's hanging like a belt, and you look at my breasts and my hips and my legs in one long glance, like you possess me, or like you might devour me, and I lie there staring back at you. I've never seen you like this, and I know it's what I wanted.

Even though time seems to freeze at that moment, it doesn't take long until you're lying on the bed, and then you make love to me, and it's a combination of the power you had in the hallway and the tenderness I always saw in your eyes, but you were too scared to put into words.

You slip yourself in me from the side, and I'm still lying on my back, with my left leg bent across your body, your right leg between mine, and you're making love to me from behind, and your hand is making slow, hypnotic circles on my clitoris, and your tongue is flicking against my nipple, interspersed with slow little bites, because you know it's the quickest way for me to come, and it is.

It doesn't take long until I start to shove myself against you, my breath quickening, and you feel my pulse start to race, and yours mimics mine, and you're pushing in harder and faster, and now you're just panting onto my breast, and I wrap my arm around you to grab you and pull you closer, and I'm shoving you while you're pressing against me, and then we're both coming at the same time, your cock somehow perfectly against my g-spot, your fingers sending a radius of pleasure across my clitoris, and I can feel your cock pulsing inside me, and it's absolutely the best sex we never had.

What I'd Like To Do To You

1. I want to play teacher. I don't know what I'm teaching, or what you're learning, but I'm sure we'll come up with something, as we sit at your desk, and we try to play serious and focus because what we're discussing is very important and we're very professional—except for every time you make a mistake, you've got to lick my pussy, and every time you get it right, I've got to lick yours.

2. I don't want to tie you up, because that's boring—I want to make you control yourself, because that's much harder. I want you to put your hands above your head, and I want to make you keep them there while I run my tongue across your clit and my fingers against your pussy, until you beg me to let you touch me, and then I pretend like I really don't know if you deserve it, until you say please and pretty please, and you're dripping all over my fingers, and then I decide that, alright, I'll let you fuck me.

3. I want to do nasty things to you under the table at your favorite restaurant, teasing and tormenting you with the light touch of my fingers on your thigh, grazing the fabric of your pants, with just enough pressure for you to moan and grip the edge of the table, until you're begging me to take you home, and throw you on the bed, and get on top, so you can feel me heavy against you, but I tell you that no, we can't leave just yet, we've got to stay and finish our meal, and then I slip my fingers between your legs, and I unzip your pants, slipping my fingers inside, underneath your underwear, between your legs, until my fingers are covered with your juices, and then while you plead with me to push harder, I pull my fingers back out and, grinning at you, run them through the food on your plate,

and then I make you lick it all off before I slide over on the seat, to get even closer, so that I can do it again, just in time for the next course.

4. I want to watch you make yourself come. I want to watch you put your hand between your legs, I want to see how you play with yourself, how you rub your clit and get yourself off. I want to see if you play with your breasts like I do, I want to see if you penetrate yourself with your fingers or if you just use a vibrator, and if you penetrate yourself with it or not. I want to sit beside and watch you, with your eyes closed, as your skin starts to glisten with sweat and your breathing starts to quicken and you tighten your legs and your chest moves up and down as little moans escape your mouth, and I don't want to make a sound because I want you to forget I'm there, and I want to watch while your body starts to spasm and you sigh, and your fingers quicken, and I can barely keep myself from touching you as your body shudders and you finally come.

5. I want to cook you dinner, but that's only an excuse to get you in the kitchen and me in an apron, with nothing underneath, just heels and some plastic wrapped around with a drawstring, pulling a June Cleaver with a twist, and you're sitting in the chair while I feed you wine, while I chop the garlic and the onions and the vegetables, and you keep trying to grab me as I walk by, but I tell you that little girls can't have dessert until they've had their dinner, and I have to keep slapping you away while you keep trying to get hold of my ass, since I told you, I'm just for show, little girls should be seen and not heard, and we drink more wine, and I finish cooking the food, but by the time it's ready, neither of us feel much like eating—at least not that kind of eating—because you've pulled me down on the floor, and I can't possibly resist anymore, since you're already between my legs, and it doesn't matter if dinner is getting cold.

6. I want to make a video, of me, getting dressed up like a

little glamour girl, high heels, dress, make-up—just the way you like it—and then taking it all off again, teasingly slowly, the way you love it, so that you can watch me, in rewind and fast-forward, dancing like a stripper, fingers on my nipples, tongue on my lips, hand between my legs, my whole body performing to make yours as hot as I can manage, and then I want to come home, and I want you to fuck me like you've spent the whole day wanting it, so that your clitoris is already swollen when I put my hand between your legs, and I can see your nipples hard against your shirt, and you don't even ask me how my day was, you just shove me against the wall and pull my damp underwear off so that you can press your fingers inside, and you tell me that I've been a very naughty girl.

7. I want to learn how you like to get fucked with a cock. I want to fuck you from behind, while you're on your hands and knees, and my hand is wrapped around your waist, flicking your clit, as I slide in and out of you, and then, as you're starting to moan, I flip you on your back, and fuck you with your legs wrapped around my waist, my tongue licking your breasts, grabbing your hips to pull me tighter, and then, because I want to be inside you when you come, I pull myself out, and slip my fingers in, instead, so that I can feel the muscles spasming around my hand, and you're grabbing my hair as you tell me it's never felt so good.

8. I want to sit on the couch with you, DVD in the player, movie on the screen, arm around your shoulder, everything easy and comfortable, until I slip my hand under the blanket, and suddenly it's not so nice anymore, it's not so sweet and domestic, because all I can hear is the sound of your breath getting faster, all I can feel is the heat coming from between your legs, and then I'm getting you off, I'm slipping my fingers in and out of you, first one then two, then one, then two again, all without moving the blanket, while the movie plays in the background but neither of us can hear it, because we just hear

171

your breath and my breath and the quiet wet sounds of my fingers sliding in and out of you, deeper and deeper, until you're grabbing the blanket between your tight fingers and your thighs are clenching, and I can feel my underwear getting wetter because nothing is hotter than you when you're about to come, and we're so distracted, it doesn't even occur to us to press pause.

9. I want to play porn star with you. I'll be the blonde and you'll be the boy. I'll wear my long blonde wig—and nothing else. You'll keep your clothes on. I'll lie on the bed while you run your fingers across my body. You'll make me spread my legs but you'll ignore what's between them, teasing me as you alternate between slipping my nipples into your hot mouth and running ice cubes over them, while they get harder, and I twist and moan, begging you to fuck me but you tell me to shut up while you keep licking and sucking and pulling and biting me until I'm red and swollen and raw, and I'm so hot and frustrated that I have to push my own fingers into my pussy which turns you on so much, you do the same thing to yourself.

10. I want to dress up like your maid at one of your parties. I don't want anyone to know who I am, or that we know each other. I want to fetch the coats, I want to serve the drinks, I want to answer the door. I want to be docile and obedient while you try not to look up my skirt, and I pretend I don't know what you look like with your clothes off. I want to move through the room as though our paths are completely separate. I want to act as though they are even though I'm aware of where you are at every second and you have to talk to everyone except me. I want to spend the whole night as your help—until everyone has left, and the last guest has left, and then we turn and look at each other, and you fuck me as your lover against the thick oak of the door.

Dahlia Schweitzer is a writer, teacher, and performer currently residing in Los Angeles.

The author of both erotic novels (LOVERGIRL, QUEEN OF HEARTS, I'VE BEEN A NAUGHTY GIRL) and cultural criticism (for outlets including HYPERALLERGIC and THE JOURNAL OF POPULAR CULTURE), Schweitzer's first academic publication, ANOTHER KIND OF MONSTER: CINDY SHERMAN'S OFFICE KILLER is published by INTELLECT PRESS via THE UNIVERSITY OF CHICAGO PRESS.

In addition to her writing, Schweitzer's critically acclaimed, recently re-released album, PLASTIQUE, consists of sexy dance music and spoken-word interludes, designed to enhance the experience of reading her books.

For more information, please visit...

www.thisisdahlia.com

www.ingramcontent.com/pod-product-compliance
Lightning Source LLC
Chambersburg PA
CBHW071249130626
46556CB00003B/1228

* 9 7 8 0 6 1 5 9 2 3 1 3 0 *